I'LL ALWAYS CHOOSE YOU

TRINITY LAKES ROMANCE
BOOK THREE

LISA RENEE

I'll Always Choose You

Book 3 Trinity Lakes Romance series

Copyright © 2023 by Lisa Renee

The Colab Press © 2023

All rights reserved.

Cover by Melissa Dalley

❀ Created with Vellum

CHAPTER ONE

J ustin Perry slipped behind the Trinity Organics shop counter and took Leah's hand in his. "When can we go on our first date?"

Leah placed a warm palm on his chest, sending instant calm to his soul. "I still need to talk to my dad."

Calmness completely ruined by one little sentence. Justin didn't let his smile waver, but his stomach twisted like a wrung-out dishrag. How absurd that Leah, at twenty-four years, still needed "daddy's approval." No one was brave or stupid enough to cross the sheriff, or Leah would be engaged already.

Mmm. The situation created a mission impossible for him too.

Leah shoed him away like a pesky fly. "You can't be behind the counter. Rhonda could walk in any minute. Then word would get back to Dad before I have a chance to plead your case."

He held his hands in surrender. "Fine." As he backed up a step, his heel met a hard surface. His body lurched forward, and his elbow knocked into a metal shelf. "Ouch." He rubbed his funny bone, which tingled in agony, but he kept the pain from showing on his face. He'd already looked like a silly goose, half-tripping over his feet. "Not much space behind here, anyway."

Leah covered her mouth, but her smile poked out from behind her fingers. "Exactly. Only room for one." She took his hand and led him to the far aisle of her organic store. Leah spun him to face her and cupped his cheeks. "Justin, I adore you. I want this relationship as much as you do. But you know what my dad's like. He'll make things difficult if we don't go about this the right way."

Justin resisted his instinct to slip his arms around her waist. Stacked shelves of organic oats, gluten-free flour, and Blitz Mix protein powders blocked the view from anyone entering the shop. He stepped into her space and got lost in her chocolate-colored eyes. The scent of her favorite lemon-myrtle shampoo curled around him. This woman was worth waiting for. All things pure and perfect. "I'll be a good boy and wait until your daddy says yes." He smirked.

Her grin was full of mischief. "Thank you. My dad and I share an unbreakable bond. No one gets him like me. And Mom, of course." Leah lifted her hands in a who-knows gesture. "Mom has the patience of a saint. Dad has a reputation for having no heart or soul, but that's the role of the sheriff. He can't be all soft on everyone. But he's a cuddly teddy bear under all that gruffness."

Justin found Leah's claim difficult to believe, but she lived with the man. Maybe the sheriff did have a softer side. Would Justin ever witness it?

The doorbell tinkled, and a gust of cool air entered the shop. Leah's eyes bulged at Justin. "Quick, get outta here."

He peeked between a packet of beetroot latte mix and turmeric powder. The long sleeves of a khaki uniform and a silver badge told him all he needed to know. He shuddered, and a wave of unease rose in his chest.

"Who is it?" Leah whispered.

The sight of the man made him sick. He moved the spices between him and the view of the door. "Not Rhonda. Worse."

Leah gritted her teeth. "Dad?"

He nodded. "Looks like I'm stuck here for a while." He groaned silently inside. "I need to get back to the workshop. I've got a kitchen to install at twelve-thirty."

"Let me handle this. Sneak out when I say the keyword."

He blinked. "And that would be?"

"I haven't figured it out yet. But you'll know."

He took her hand and risked a quick kiss on her knuckles. Gotta keep the romance going, even though he wasn't allowed to date her yet. Sheesh. Why did he pick the sheriff's daughter to fall in love with?

Leah spun around and flounced toward the front of the shop. She stopped for a second and glanced over her shoulder, giving him a broad smile, cheeks dimpling before she disappeared. That was why he'd fallen for her. Leah was the epitome of elegance and grace. If he had to wait seven years and herd sheep in a deserted pasture, he'd do it.

Hold on. How'd the Bible story go? Man, that dude got a tough deal. Jacob worked seven years for Rachel, only to be ripped off and had to work another seven years. Good thing Leah didn't have an older sister. And his Leah sure wasn't weak on the eyes. She was gorgeous. How she was single was a mystery. Although, when her dad came into the equation, perhaps it wasn't such a head-scratcher.

"Daddy, what are you doing here?" Leah's voice came out all chipper.

"Came to see my little girl." The sheriff's voice boomed across the store.

Justin's stomach lurched, not from jealousy but something else. The man smothered Leah, but Justin couldn't tell her that. She adored her father and only viewed him in a positive light. If Justin wanted a future with Leah, he also needed to win the sheriff's heart. His throat constricted like someone had him in a death grip. Never had he seen the sheriff so much as crack a smile at him. They'd never exchanged so much as a single full sentence of conversation. Was it because of the past? Sure, Justin had made a mistake as a teenager and lost his license for two years. It had been a harsh lesson, but sixteen was a decade ago. He was a new man now. As far as he was concerned—as far as God was concerned—the past had been washed away in the Pacific Ocean.

"Great that you popped in," Leah said. "I need a hand with a delivery out the back. They stacked the buckets too high. I'll be fine with the rest if you could lower the fifty-pound coconut sugar from the top."

"Anything for you, cupcake."

Ugh.

The sheriff's shoes clicked against the tiled floor.

Justin crouched and crab-crawled to the end of the aisle, ready to make a run for the front door. The bell would jingle when he opened it, so he needed to wait a little longer, until the sheriff was out of hearing. The sense of urgency increased his heart rate, and his palms dripped in sweat.

"Won't take a minute, Dad." Leah practically yelled the words —his cue to scram the heck out of there.

In one minute, the sheriff would be in the back warehouse.

A pang of disappointment hit Justin. He shouldn't have to sneak around, hiding his budding relationship with Leah. At first, he'd admired her at church from a distance. They'd become friends through the young adult group. But he was twenty-six now, and Leah was only two years younger. Surely they could officially date. He saw a future with her, and only one obstacle stood in his way—the grumpy sheriff of Trinity Lakes, the man everyone tiptoed around.

———

LEAH THOMPSON GLANCED over her shoulder as her father followed her past the storage room toward the roller doors where the delivery driver had left the containers. "How much time do you have?"

Dad lifted one shoulder, his hands resting on his belt. "Nothing too urgent in sleepy Trinity Lakes. I'll get a call if I'm needed." He strode up beside her, his tall and muscular frame blocking the outside light. "Loads of paperwork, but I'll be home for dinner. Who is cooking tonight? You or your mother?"

Leah took a deep breath of the chilly air emanating from the concrete walls. "I might go out for dinner. Justin is hoping to take me somewhere nice."

Dad's eyes narrowed into slits as his voice came out sharp. "Justin Perry?" He straightened and propped a hand on his gun. "You mean on a date?"

Leah pushed an empty box with her sneaker away from the stack of powders. "Yeah. I like him, and he likes me. That's what single young people do, Dad. If they like each other, they spend time together."

"Humph. I could tell you a thing or two about Justin." His lips tightened into a stern line. "But I can't expose certain information."

Leah swung around and faced her father. "What are you talking about? Are you saying he broke the law? Justin isn't a criminal." Her fists clenched at her sides. "He goes to church and helps with the youth group. He's a good man."

Dad's lips twitched. His gaze darted about the warehouse as he rubbed his nose with his index finger. "Dusty out back. You need to air this place out. Leave the roller doors up for a while."

Leah resisted huffing out her frustration. She studied the exposed beams as dust flittered in the fluorescent light. "Yeah, I'll do that."

"Just not while you're alone in the shop. Don't want

someone coming in without you knowing and absconding with your stock."

"Understood." She pointed to the top container. "I need that one down, please. Be careful, or they all might topple. Then I'll be driving your police car to get you to a hospital, sirens blasting."

He gave her a wink before cracking a joke. "You of little faith."

Why did Dad show his fun and soft side to her and Mom, but he barely smiled at others? No one believed that Dad had a caring side. Sure, he was overprotective, but that overprotective nature made him a good sheriff, husband, and father. Yet Dad had something on Justin that couldn't be disclosed. Was it something from when Justin was a juvenile? That had to be it. Otherwise, Dad would've told her by now because it would have been a matter of public record.

What had happened in his past that caused Dad to have a grudge against Justin? She needed to confront Justin and find out. If she didn't know the whole truth, she couldn't and wouldn't take their relationship any further.

CHAPTER TWO

Justin cruised down Wainscott Drive, his elbow propped out of the open window as his hair whipped in the wind. The largest lake in town glistened glassy blue from the morning sun and bright sky. In the distance, the mountains blurred in soft earth tones mixed with shades of purple, dotted with evergreen pines that crested above the horizon.

He passed a parking lot where an older lady cupped her hands to a car window. Justin took his foot off the gas and craned his neck toward the side mirror. Peppered hair, rolled shoulders, and a glittery cardigan—Olivia Darcy. Was everything okay?

He directed his pickup in a wide circle easily enough with no other traffic to block him. He parked beside Mrs. Darcy's vintage BMW. He jumped out, but the woman didn't notice him.

Jiggling the car handle, Mrs. Darcy huffed. "Stupid. Stupid."

"I hope you're not talking about me." Justin came around the trunk and stood before her.

She straightened as much as her rolled shoulders would allow and offered a half smile. "Never. But I'm a silly sausage for locking my keys in the car. If my grandson finds out, it'll prove his point that I shouldn't be driving at my age." Deep lines creased her forehead. "He's right, you know."

Justin waved a hand. "Nonsense. All ages lock keys in their car on occasion. Let me see if I can help."

Mrs. Darcy dropped her hands to her sides. "You are a dear. Thank you, Justin." She flapped her blouse. "I'm getting all hot and bothered over this. Do you mind if I sit on the bench down by the lake? I need to do some breathing exercises and calm down."

He lifted his hands. "Go for it. The lake always makes me feel relaxed. I'll come and get you when I've finished."

"God bless you, son." She turned and headed toward the picnic area.

Justin returned to his utility, popped open his toolbox, and pulled out a metal tray. What would be thin enough to slide into the locking system? He dug around his tools but couldn't find what he needed. Where was a wired clothes hanger or a metal ruler when it was needed to break into a car? He closed his toolbox and rummaged in the glove compartment. Perfect. Old sunglasses with a thin rim tumbled to the floor, along with his car manual and random envelopes. He'd forgotten about those bills.

He scooped the spare sunglasses from the car mat. They'd only cost fifteen dollars and helping an old lady was worth every cent. The poor woman seemed flustered. Did her grandson give her a hard time about her forgetfulness?

Justin quickly got to work and jammed the metal frame between the window and the car door toward the locking system. Would the little hook reach where it needed to go? He'd never had to break into a car before. His line about everyone locking their keys in their car at least once might be an exaggeration. He'd only seen this done in the movies. But if a man couldn't work out something this simple, what use was he in emergencies?

Justin raised his elbow and pressed his thigh into the door, trying to get a better angle.

Blue and red lights flashed in his peripheral vision. No sirens.

Fan-freaking-tastic. The sheriff. Way to make an impression on the father of the woman of his dreams. He jumped back from the car. The glasses poked out at a crooked angle, stuck in the gap of the window frame.

Justin swung his hands behind his back, not looking guilty at all. He resisted whistling. That would be way too obvious. Before the sheriff could get out of his car, Justin stepped past the trunk, pasted on a fake grin, and waved like one of those happy clowns at a circus. Almost laughable.

His throat tightened as the sheriff stepped from his vehicle with a frown on his face. "Justin. Up to your old tricks again, I see."

Huh? Justin raised his palms and clenched his jaw. "Just helping out a little old lady."

In two strides, Sheriff Thompson grabbed Justin's wrist, spun him in a circle, and thrust his arm up his back.

Ouch.

The wind left his lungs as the sheriff shoved him against the car's trunk and pushed his head into the metal. "Justin Perry, you're under arrest."

"But I did nothing wrong." He mumbled with his cheek squashed to Mrs. Darcy's trunk.

The sheriff pushed his arm higher. "You have the right to remain silent …" The sheriff recited the familiar words Justin had often heard on television but hadn't heard in real life for the best part of a decade.

The click of handcuffs and cold metal against his wrists made this nightmare real.

"I'm taking you to the station for questioning." The sheriff's voice came out low and grumbly.

"You can ask me questions here." Justin craned his neck toward the BMW. "Check the ignit—"

Sheriff Thompson jerked him away, cutting off his protest. Pain shot through Justin's forearm as the sheriff rough-handled him into the police car.

Wait until Leah heard about this one. It would prove her father was over the top and had a personal vendetta against him. Ridiculous.

The lake glided by in sharp blue, sailboats and kayaks dotting its surface. Just great. Everyone and their dog were out today in this beautiful weather. Justin slumped down in the seat until most of his head was below the window. The last thing he needed was to be seen in the back of a police cruiser. Gossip in this town spread like wildfire. He closed his eyes and voiced a silent prayer. *God, please help me through this mess.*

JUSTIN SAT in an unfamiliar antiseptic room filled with cameras and neon lights that cast an eerie glow on the solemn faces of Sheriff Thompson and another cop, someone Justin didn't know. Cold white walls boxed them in around a melamine table with a microphone in the middle. The intimidating cameras pointed down as though Justin was in the middle of a criminal investigation.

Sheriff Thompson shuffled papers and wrote a few notes. The microphone squawked when he tapped it with a pen. The sheriff narrowed his eyes at Justin, "I can call Olivia Darcy to validate your claims, but I'll put you in the cell until I can confirm your statement." The sheriff sighed as though he was tired of this whole rigmarole.

The tension in Justin's neck worsened. No point in arguing

further, so he simply said, "I'm telling the truth." Why wouldn't the man believe him?

The sheriff huffed. He pulled out his phone, searched, and dialed Mrs. Darcy's number before switching it to loudspeaker. "Let's see if she confirms your story."

Justin sat still and waited, counting the seconds as the phone rang on the other end.

Mumbles of conversation and the clicking of heels on polished concrete flitted down the hallway of the police station. It sounded like Mrs. Darcy, and was that Liam's posh accent? Thank the Lord. They had come to his rescue. The poor woman must've ended up calling her grandson. Had she seen Justin's arrest?

Another police officer, Darius Mitchell, entered the room. "Sheriff, Liam Darcy is here to see you. It's true. Olivia Darcy had locked her keys in the car. Liam had a spare set at home, and Mrs. Darcy wants to see Justin immediately to clear this matter up."

The sheriff's face went pale, then flushed pink. Not a pretty pink like his daughter, but one which highlighted his sunspots.

Sheriff turned to Justin. "You stay here, and I'll get a statement from Mrs. Darcy. Looks like you won't need to go into the cell."

Justin resisted an eye roll. "Thank you, sir."

Both police officers followed the sheriff down the hallway. Once they were out of sight, Justin stood and craned his neck to get a better hearing.

Mrs. Darcy's voice seemed flustered. "How dare you accuse an innocent man. Justin was only doing what I asked him to."

Liam interrupted. "Calm down, Grandma. The sheriff is just doing his job. Stick to the facts."

"All right. I locked my keys in my car, and Justin was kind enough to pull over and see what he could do so I didn't have to bother Liam. I went to rest on the picnic bench because I was hot and frustrated with myself. Then I heard a commotion, and I tried to get up the slope of the grass bank. Then I witnessed you, Sheriff Thompson, who won't be getting my vote next election—"

Justin bit back a laugh.

"—manhandling Justin into the police car. You handcuffed him and treated him terribly."

"Gran." Liam drew the word out, as if in warning.

"Right. Anyway, Justin did nothing wrong." Mrs. Darcy's tone was strident. "Release him immediately, or I'll call my lawyer."

Justin made a mental note to never annoy Olivia Darcy.

Sheriff's voice lowered, and Justin leaned further past the door frame but couldn't make out the words. The sheriff would have to eat humble pie. Maybe he'd feel bad enough that he'd let Justin date his daughter.

Justin scurried back to the uncomfortable chair and sat rubbing the back of his neck. Would the sheriff apologize?

Several minutes later, Officer Darius Mitchell reentered the room. "You're free to go now."

Justin widened his eyes. "Is Sheriff Thompson coming to speak to me first?"

Darius shook his head. "No need. He's got paperwork to do."

"Do I need to sign anything?"

"Don't worry about it. We'll just pretend this little incident didn't happen."

Justin scraped his chair back and stood. "Never happened? So no apology, then?"

Darius tilted his head, and his brows angled inward. "You think you'll get an apology from the sheriff? Lake Wainscott will turn to lava before that happens."

CHAPTER THREE

Leah stood over the stove and stirred the pot of beef stew, allowing the heat to warm her chin. The aroma of onion and garlic filled her nostrils.

Mom handed her a saltshaker filled with pink Himalayan salt. "It could do with a little more." Mom's sweet smile made Leah smile as well.

"Thanks. Hey, did Dad say how long he was going to be? I timed dinner so it'd be ready when he usually gets home."

"He hasn't called to say he'll be late. I hope everything is okay. No matter how many years he's been working in the police force, I tend to worry. Not so much in a small town, but still." Mom shrugged.

"I'm sure he'll walk in the door any minute."

"Of course." Mom retrieved some cutlery. "How was business today?"

"Good. It's always a little slow at the beginning of the week. But the orders from the country club are picking up. They're adding some organic items to their menu to be more upmarket. Not for health reasons, but because organic is trendy."

"Right."

"The chef wants to do spicy roasted almonds. He creates the spice blend himself. Thinks he's Colonel Sanders, and no one can know the recipe. He bulk-ordered a month's supply of organic almonds. Then I have a few deliveries for healthy snacks at the rowing club. I have Hannah to thank for that order."

Mom tapped her forefinger to her temple. "Like they say, it's not what you know, but *who* you know."

"Sure helps. Melanie and Adam's Blitz Mixes are doing well now they're manufactured locally. It used to take weeks to get here from Australia, and the shipping costs were a killer. He sends his physiotherapy clients to buy his product through me rather than selling directly."

"That's nice of him. I like Adam." Mom set three placemats on the dining table. "It all sounds lovely, hon. How close are you to paying off your loan?"

"Nearly there. Then I can move out of home and get out of your hair."

Mom came over and placed a hand on Leah's shoulder. "Baby, we love having you here. I'm gonna cry myself silly when you move out. You can stay here until you get married."

"When's that going to happen? Dad doesn't think anyone in this little town is good enough."

"Your father only wants the best for you." Mom squeezed, then dropped her hand. "I want the best for you. You're a classy lady and shouldn't settle for second best." She wagged a finger. "You don't need lots of boyfriends, just that special one. Waiting is better than getting married too soon and the relationship ending in a divorce. It might take you until you're thirty to meet that person. Some young people marry at thirty-five."

Leah choked out a laugh. "I can't live at home at thirty-five, that's for sure."

Mom grinned. "I guess we'd have to let you go before then."

She brushed Leah's forearm. "I'll set the table." Mom headed to the cabinet and took out three side plates.

Leah wasn't even close to thirty, but it still was time to move out. Having cozy little dinners, just the three of them, was all too familiar with being the only child. She was close to her parents, but maybe one of the Bible college students would want to stay in Trinity Lakes and go halves in rent with her. It was a blessing that her parents had let her stay rent-free while she set up her organic business. Trinity Organics cost thousands to fit out the warehouse with shelving, install a cool room, and buy stock. So much went into starting a business from scratch.

The door clicked open and heavy footsteps came from the front of the house.

"Sorry I'm late." Dad stepped into the kitchen area and kissed Mom on the cheek. "Smells good in here."

Mom smiled and looked at Leah. "Our girl has made a delicious certified organic beef stew."

"Must be expensive, then."

Leah waved. "I had some leftover produce and couldn't let it go to waste. So I cooked up a big batch. We'll have enough leftovers for lunches for the next three days."

Dad pulled a chair back, sat, and placed his palms on the table. "Well, I'm starved. Organic or not, I'll eat anything right now."

Leah came around the kitchen counter, and Mom placed bowls next to the side dishes. Leah scooped a large portion of stew into each bowl and brought over the crusty bread and freshly whipped butter. She settled into a seat after Mom sat.

"So, Dad, how was your day?"

Dad coughed and spluttered.

Mom patted his back. "Are you okay, hon?"

Leah stood. "I'll get you a drink."

Dad flapped his hand and coughed into his fist. "I'm fine. Sit down." It was more of a command than a suggestion. Dad had that edge to him sometimes.

"I'm surprised you're here tonight, Leah. Weren't you going on a date?"

Mom looked at Leah with question in her eyes. "A date?"

Leah shook her head at her parents. "Dad, you said you didn't want me to go out with Justin. Wouldn't you be upset if I had?"

Dad leaned back in his chair and gripped the side of the table. "I didn't say you couldn't go out with him. I just think you could do better. A lot better." Dad huffed. "He'll probably tell you what happened today."

Leah's pulse quickened. "What happened?"

"It's nothing to worry about, but to summarize the event, I saw him fiddling with a car and thought he was breaking in."

Leah's mouth dropped, and Mom gasped.

Dad dipped his chin. "It was a misunderstanding. I was simply doing my duty and ensuring everything was above-board." He frowned at Leah. "But he might be annoyed with me."

"He shouldn't be annoyed if you're just doing your job."

Dad clapped his hands. "Exactly. So be careful of his twisted version of the story. I'm telling you first. When I see someone acting suspiciously, I'm required to follow protocol and take them down to the station for questioning."

"You took him to the station?" Leah covered her mouth.

"I needed to record his statement. Wasn't going to do it in the parking lot, was I?"

"Of course not."

Dad scooted his chair closer to the table and collected his spoon. "No big deal. Another day where people get frustrated and don't like me because I'm the sheriff."

Mom rubbed his shoulder. "Honey, someone needs to do your job. And people do like you. They like that you protect the town. You can't be all soft with everyone or be everyone's friend."

Dad nodded once. "Yeah, I don't need lots of friends. My work colleagues understand me. And my girls." Dad looked intently into Leah's eyes. "You're precious, and I want to protect you. You're my number one priority above all of Trinity Lakes. Being a sheriff comes second to my role as a husband to your mother and a father to you." Dad brushed Leah's nose. "You're my number one priority. And I don't want anything. Anyone. To hurt you. You understand?"

She nodded.

"That's why I want you to trust me when I have an instinct about someone. Your mother and I pray for you every day. We've prayed for you since you were in the womb, and we've raised you right. We don't want you getting involved with the wrong guy."

"I don't want that either. I won't date just any John Doe." Leah took a bite of the stew. The shredded meat broke easily between her teeth. Warm liquid slipped down her throat.

Dad took a bite of his, then placed a spoon on the table. "Instead of dating Justin, why don't you date other guys first?"

Leah nearly bit her tongue. Dad had never said anything like this before. His advice was usually to wait for that special one. Now he was suggesting she go out with several men? That didn't make sense. Mom's forehead creased showing she was equally confused.

"You want me to date lots of people."

"Not kissing them or anything. Go for lunch or dinner or a picnic. I don't know what young people do these days." He scowled. "But no touchy-feely stuff. Just get to know them as a friend. Surely there are more eligible bachelors in Trinity Lakes than Justin Perry." He put on his pleading puppy-dog look, big brown eyes and all. "Please, respect my wishes and date more widely before you decide to start anything with Justin. Trust me on this. There's something I know about him that I can't talk about. And I feel Justin isn't the man for you."

Leah's insides contracted. She liked Justin and saw the best in him. He made her laugh, relax, and feel alive. But Dad wouldn't be saying these things unless there was some truth to it. He was a man of God—said he prayed, loved, and cared for her.

Maybe she was too emotionally involved with Justin and couldn't see his flaws. Maybe Dad was right. Perhaps they should stay friends, and if the opportunity came to date someone else first, then at least she could say she had tried.

———

JUSTIN SCANNED his surroundings at the Bellbird Café. Sure, it had a cozy atmosphere, but it seemed chaotic at times. Tables were precariously balanced with folded pieces of cardboard under some of the legs, and chairs stood at different heights, which scrambled his carpentry brain.

The wooden floors would wobble if you so much as looked at them. The tealight candles were a nice touch, but they were haphazardly placed in odd containers. Large plates painted with random designs hung on the sunshine-yellow walls, the complex patterns leaving Justin questioning the artist's sanity. Shelves lined with vintage teacups and teapots completed the mismatched look.

Brandon and Josh were talking about cars again. He hadn't seen Brandon at the combined churches' YA meetups for a while, so he had tried to catch up with him. Although Justin wasn't a young adult leader, he still had a heart for Brandon. The guy lived on the edge.

Leah entered the cafe with Melanie. Justin jerked and hit his knee under the table.

Josh frowned at him. "You all right, man?"

"Yeah, just saw someone I want to talk to."

Josh glanced over his shoulder. "Still haven't gone on a date with her?"

"No. She wanted to talk to her dad first."

"Seriously?" Brandon shook his head. "She's twenty-four. She doesn't need her dad's permission."

"It's not that she needs his permission. She wants his blessing, or he'll make things harder for us."

Josh nodded. His parents were pastors, so he got the whole honor-your-parents thing.

Leah made her way to the counter, oblivious to his presence.

As she walked by, he leaned across the table to tap her hand, but his foot caught on the table's leg. He slipped from his seat, and his knee cracked on the floor.

Leah jumped back and bumped into Melanie. They both stared at Justin, half lying on the floor, rubbing his kneecap.

"Hey, fancy seeing you here." Justin offered his most charming grin.

"Oh boy." Melanie bit her lip, her cheeks puffing as she eyed her friend.

Leah held out a hand. "You want some help?"

Justin didn't take the offer but pushed himself up and dusted the back of his jeans. "Can we talk?"

Leah's forehead creased. "I'm with Melanie at the moment. Do you want to join us?"

He glanced between the girls and shrugged.

Melanie shifted on her feet. "You two find a table, and I'll order." She turned to Leah. "The usual?"

"Yeah, thanks. I'll transfer some money to your account."

Melanie waved a hand down. "Don't worry about it. Justin, can I get you anything?"

"I've eaten. But thanks."

Melanie smiled and headed to the serving counter.

Leah pointed to an empty booth. "Do you want to sit over there? Is this going to take long?"

Okay. She wasn't as warm and friendly as usual. Maybe the talk with her father didn't go as planned. He nodded and followed her to a table. He sat, and the air squeezing out of the vinyl cushion created a rude squeak. His neck heated even though Leah would know it was the chair.

She sat across from him and threaded her fingers. "What's up?"

"That's my question. How did things go with your dad? Did you talk to him about us?"

Her chest rose and fell, and her lashes flittered to the bright ceiling. "Kind of. I mentioned going to dinner with you, and he wasn't thrilled. Let's put it that way."

"But he won't stop you from going out with me? Right?"

"Um ..."

She paused for so long that Justin thought she'd forgotten the question.

"He said I should date other men first."

Other men? Men, not one man. How many men did the sheriff think Leah should date? And who was she supposed to date? The sheriff had already scared off all the eligible men in Trinity Lakes.

"And you think this is a good idea?" Justin lifted his gaze to lock eyes with Leah.

"He's trying to do the right thing by me. You know, to make sure I'm sure."

Justin rubbed the back of his neck. "Sure that I'm worthy of you?"

Leah patted his left hand. "Justin, you're a good man." She leaned back. "I guess Dad doesn't want me to settle for the first guy who likes me."

Several guys had liked Leah in the past, but the sheriff had scared them all away.

"Leah, I don't want to see you with other guys. That would be uncomfortable. I thought we had something special."

Leah rested her elbows on the table. "I do like you. A lot. If I do what my dad suggests, he'll feel better—he'll feel like I've kept my options open, and I'm not rushing into anything."

"You're twenty-four, and we've known each other for years. We're not rushing." More like a snail inching toward the altar, and its shell had become too small a long time ago.

"I know, I know, but I haven't really dated anyone."

He resisted blurting out, *and there's a reason for that.* It wouldn't look good if he put down her father, the man she idolized.

Justin rubbed his forehead. "All right. Can you do me a favor, though? Don't date anyone else yet. Let me think about it. I'll come up with a plan. Maybe I need to talk to your dad myself. Ask for his permission or something."

Leah shook her head. "Seems like that won't work." She glanced around the room. A waitress delivered a plate of food to the people behind them. Leah leaned in "I heard he arrested you the other day," she whispered.

"Yes. He didn't even let me speak. Twisted my arm and shoved me into Mrs. Darcy's car, which was uncalled for."

"It's procedure. He needed to take you to the station for questioning. You looked like you were breaking into a car. What else was he meant to do?"

Justin ground his molars. "He could've listened to me. Let me actually speak for a second. Then I could have called out to Mrs. Darcy to confirm I was helping her out. She was down by the lake."

Leah's lips thinned. "I don't need to stand up for my dad. That's between you and him and what happened the other day. But I can see that he has something against you." She crossed her arms. "Do you know why that might be?"

Justin scraped his teeth on his bottom lip. What was Leah

talking about? "I was a bit of a rascal when I was a teenager, but that's years ago."

"Could it be anything else? More recent?"

"No. You've known me for years. Nothing goes unnoticed in this town. If there were something secret, it wouldn't be secret for long. Not with people like Rhonda."

Melanie approached the table and sat beside Leah.

Justin tapped the table. "All right, ladies. I'll let you get back to whatever you're going to talk about." He felt about as awkward as a wrestler in a toddler's highchair. "I'll make my way back over there." He stood and pointed his thumb over his shoulder.

Leah giggled. "Okay. Well, let me know when you come up with your plan. Can't wait to hear your ideas."

Justin pointed his finger like a gun. "Exactly. I'm the man with a plan. I just need to come up with one and execute said plan."

Melanie burst out laughing.

"Glad I could offer some entertainment." He stood and pointed over his shoulder. "My boys need me." Justin turned on his heel and headed back to his friends. He imagined Melanie and Leah staring at his back, holding in their laughter until he was out of earshot.

How would he come up with a master plan?

CHAPTER FOUR

Justin walked beside one of the summer camp counselors, Ryan Kozlanski, into the food hall. Gray-blue walls held group photos of campers, past and present. If only Justin could Photoshop the one showing him as a lanky zit-faced teenager. So glad he'd literally grown out of that phase.

As they made their way past the empty buffet tables, Justin had a vivid memory of a food fight he'd been part of. He smiled at the memory but quickly forgot his train of thought when he entered the commercial-grade kitchen.

Two men in chef's uniforms stood hunched over a frying pan, their expressions as intense as the vent hood blowing on high. Ryan gestured toward the men. "That's the Australian team—some of them, anyway."

Justin studied the men with admiration. He'd always been fascinated with the cooking process but wasn't motivated to learn anything past bacon and eggs or a few basic meals. Maybe he could volunteer in the kitchen this year.

Ryan drew closer to the men, who seemed to be in a heated discussion about the right amount of paprika to add to the mix.

Ryan nodded as they greeted him, but he didn't interrupt their debate. He just watched, a hint of a smile on his lips.

He turned to Justin and gestured to the chefs. "They sure are passionate about their craft."

"What are they doing, cooking already? Camp is two weeks away."

"They're probably cooking for their crew and the new leader training starts a week before. We certainly won't be providing gourmet food for hundreds of teenagers. Blast our budget to outer space."

"We can't have that." Justin tugged on his T-shirt as he took in the sight of the muscle-bound chef on the right. The guy must be over six feet tall. His shoulders were as wide as a mini truck, and a neck tattoo peeked from his collar. Justin squinted but couldn't work out the design.

The other man turned and waved. "Hey, you've arrived just in time. We cooked extra." He had an American accent, but from what state?

Justin twitched his mouth to the side and whispered to Ryan, "I thought you said they were Australian."

"Chris married an Australian. He did summer camps here years ago, but now has his own restaurant in Australia."

Ryan waved as they approached the kitchen.

The big guy seemed much younger—probably in his early twenties. When he turned, his shirt stretched across his taut chest. He must spend hours in the gym to get muscles like that.

The chef with grays in his sideburns held out his hand. "I'm Chris Evanson."

Justin shook Chris's hand. He had kind brown eyes.

Chris gestured to the guy beside him. "This is Marcus. It's his first time out of Australia. He started working with me when he was sixteen and has won several awards already in his short career."

"Gee. Shucks, boss." Marcus elbowed Chris.

Marcus held out his meaty hand, and Justin shook it. The guy had a death grip, but his smile remained broad and friendly —just a strong dude.

"Nice to meet you. How's your first experience in America? Not too weird?"

He nodded slowly. "I'm diggin' it. The food is so-so." He shook his hands in a seesaw motion. "But Chris and I are here now, so it's all under control." He clapped his hands.

Ryan laughed. "I'm not sure about that, not on our small budget."

Marcus held up his forefinger. "Chris and I have been talking, and this will be the best summer camp food yet. We know how to make anything taste amazing. It's all in the secret sauce." Marcus winked at Chris.

"Doesn't have MSG, does it?" Justin asked. Leah would be proud of his question.

Chris jerked his head back. "No way. We don't use flavor enhancers. That's cheating."

"You'd get along with my girlfriend." Justin shifted his weight to his other foot. "Well, she's not my girlfriend, but my friend who's a girl." He didn't dare look at Ryan. "She owns Trinity Organics and always goes on about synthetic chemicals. Artificial colors and flavors."

Chris chuckled. "My wife's the same, but I'm glad she's health conscious now we have a little one. I don't want any of that genetically modified frankenfood. We're organic all the way when it comes to our toddler."

Justin nodded. "If there is anything we can help you with, you let us know."

"We're good for now." Marcus grinned. "We wanted to see the setup here, and then we're gonna do a little touring in Walla Walla and the surrounding areas."

Chris smiled. "We'll return a few days before camp and get everything in order."

"I'm able to leave the workshop early if you want to go fishing or anything around here. We have some great rivers and lakes here. Kayaking. Water sports."

Chris massaged his chin. "Sounds good."

Justin scanned Marcus from his chef beret to his steel-toe-capped boots. "You look like you're into the gym. We have one local."

Chris laughed and smacked Marcus's back, but the guy didn't move. "Yeah, you could say that."

Marcus glanced at his boss and back to Justin. "I do heavy weightlifting. I'm gonna be in a championship when I return to Australia, so I need to keep up my fitness."

"What kind of heavy weightlifting do you do?"

"Crazy stuff. Have you ever seen those videos where they drag car bodies using giant chains?"

Justin frowned. "What the heck? No."

"Imagine an old, rusted-out car with no engine and no wheels. Chains connected like ropes, and they strap around your chest and shoulders. You've got to drag it over the finish line. The fastest bloke wins."

"That's heavy duty. Literally."

Marcus gripped his shoulder and squeezed. "You're a funny guy. We should hang out. I could show you how to get buff like me, mate. Make that female friend of yours become your real girlfriend."

Bubbles of laughter rose from his belly. Justin threw his head back and allowed his laughter to echo throughout the room. "I'm not sure if that will win Leah over, but I guess it couldn't hurt."

A crazy idea popped into Justin's head. He studied the neck tattoo. Japanese writing? Sheriff Thompson would totally freak out if Leah dated someone like Marcus. A plan started to form in his mind. Marcus seemed like the kind of guy who liked to have some fun. Maybe they could become "mates," as he called it, and Marcus could do him a favor in exchange for some tourism.

———

LEAH unscrewed the lid from the gluten-free flour dispenser and poured in a new batch. Particles puffed into the air and tickled her nostrils. She twisted her head out of the way. Breathing from the side of her mouth, she shook the bag of the last bit of flour and shut the lid. Leah pressed the back of her hand to her nose, resisting a sneeze.

The doorbell tinkled. She folded the recycled paper bag and glanced over her shoulder to find a handsome man strolling toward her. Justin. Every time she saw him, her breath hitched. His eyes lit up like they did when he saw her across the room at church, like she was the only person in the room. She'd never seen him looking at another girl in that way. He'd been like this for years, but in the last few weeks, it was as if he'd decided their relationship needed to move forward.

"Hi." Her voice croaked.

"Hey, yourself." He wriggled his fingers toward the crinkled paper. "Can I put that in the trash for you?"

"Oh, sure. The can is behind the counter."

"I know where it is and every part of this shop. It's my favorite place in Trinity Lakes."

Aw. Justin was such a sweetheart, and he meant every word. She circled her forefinger and playfully poked his chest. "You just like the free samples."

His smile came easy. "That's not the only thing I want to sample. When do I get to sample those lips of yours?"

Her mouth dropped open. "You're unbelievable." She placed the brown bag into his hands. The pad of his thumb brushed her skin, sending tingles up her arm. His mouth turned upward, and she blinked. Oh, gosh. She'd been staring at his lips. And he knew it.

Justin took the bag slowly from her and raised a brow. "I'll dispose of this and be right back." As he passed her, she breathed in his familiar scent. A mix of something like cinnamon and pine, but he probably didn't use organic after-shave. If they were dating, she'd buy him some.

She turned and followed him. "Would you like a chocolate energy ball?"

"Now you're talking. I love those."

She nibbled on her fingernail. No one else was in the store, and a magnetic field drew her toward Justin. They'd known each other for a long time, but recently things had shifted. She didn't want to date other guys. She only wanted Justin. But while living under her dad's roof, she respected his wishes and listened to his wise counsel. That was what the logic side of her brain told her. The emotional, impractical side said she should throw caution to the wind, wrap her arms around this hunky man and kiss him senseless. Oh boy. She had it bad.

"What are you thinking? You have a mischievous look."

"Me?" She pointed to herself. "Mischievous? The sheriff's daughter? Never." She crossed her arms. "But you can talk, mister. Have you come up with a plan yet?"

He pressed his foot to the trash can and squashed the paper bag into the can. Justin straightened and raised his index finger. "I have a master plan starting with a master chef."

She tilted her head. "A chef?"

"Not just any chef. A neck-tattooed Australian chef."

Leah scrunched her face. "Huh? What's he got to do with you and me?"

"This is going to be hilarious." Justin clapped his hands and bounced on his sneakers. "I've met this awesome guy. He's so cool. He's as big as an army truck and has a neck tattoo." He gestured toward his throat. "What if your dad thought you might fall in love with this Australian guy?" Justin leaned forward, and his eyes grew wide. "If you did fall in love with him, your dad could lose you forever to Australia."

Leah jolted back like he'd zapped her with a taser. "Oh my gosh. That is brilliant."

Justin nodded slowly. "I'm not just a pretty face. I'm a genius."

Leah touched her belly and laughed. "When do I get to meet this… army truck, Australian chef?"

"I need him to agree first. Marcus seems easygoing, so I can't see why he wouldn't. He's away sightseeing for a few days. But I'll confirm when I visit the campgrounds next. Then I can introduce you, and we'll finalize a plan. Until then, tell your dad you've taken to heart what he said about dating other men. And you've met this amazing guy who can cook." Justin waved a hand. "Don't give him too many details. Spring it on him later. Randomly turn up somewhere with Marcus on your arm."

She rubbed her chin. "What if I invited him to a family dinner? Tell Dad I wanted him to meet Marcus first to see what he thinks."

Justin touched his chest. "And I thought I was the genius. You're a mastermind. Together, we can take over the world." He raised one arm in the air, fingers crooked, and let out a silly cackle as if all the power had gone to his head.

No wonder all the youth loved him. She nearly jumped into his arms as excitement bubbled within her. But they weren't at that stage in their relationship.

Justin dug his hands into his back pockets. Did he feel the same way? They couldn't hug each other—someone would see and tell Dad, and he'd flip out—but they both wanted to.

"Have Marcus come to your house for dinner. He'll have the worst table manners. Love all the things your dad hates. We'll have to brainstorm, but this could be a lot of fun." He took her hand. "This will be a great story to tell our kids and grandkids one day."

Leah stilled and held her breath. Justin wanted to marry her. He was that kind of guy, and she was that kind of girl. What would it be like to be married to Justin Perry? He cared about young people and had a generous heart. And he knew how to have fun.

Justin dropped her hand. "Everything okay? I'm getting ahead of myself, aren't I?"

She gave a nervous chuckle. "Speaking of the future, when will you apply for the youth leader position?" The church had funding now and needed a youth leader on staff. Justin was the perfect candidate. If only he believed in himself as she did.

CHAPTER FIVE

The sun dipped lower to the horizon, its rays spanning over Lake Other. The camp volunteers huddled under a canopy tent, engaging in devotions before their training and preparation for summer camp.

Several yards away, Justin assisted the cooking crew for lunch. His mouth watered as Marcus flipped another hamburger. Oil hissed as it hit the hot grill. Marcus worked at ease, oblivious to the heat, while the man's precise movements transfixed Justin in a daze.

"Can I help somehow?" Justin asked. He was no Gordon Ramsey, but he could flip a burger.

"I've got it sorted." Marcus flicked his gaze toward the gathering and the leader sharing from the Bible. "Chris wants me to listen and take it all in. He'll be wondering if I did." He switched the metal spatula to his other hand and sucked on his finger where some oil had spattered.

Justin grinned and kept busy setting the table beside him.

Chris approached and whispered to Marcus, "Meeting will close in ten minutes. Better get the hotdogs on."

"You mean sausages, mate." Marcus winked.

Marcus made room on the grill for rows of link sausages made from beef and apparently a traditional barbeque staple in Australia. Justin breathed in the aroma of sauteed onions. He should've had breakfast. Then he wouldn't be drooling.

He distracted himself by focusing on the green waters of the enormous lake, reflecting the mountain landscape and a distant bridge.

But then Marcus piled a serving tray with burger patties, covered it in foil, and placed it on a trestle table behind them. Justin's hunger pains returned, even stronger.

At one end of the table, Kyla buttered sandwich bread for the sausages and onions—something Marcus assured him was how they ate this typical Aussie tucker. Justin had caught Kyla eying Marcus's neck tattoo earlier and scrunching her button nose. Another reason that she didn't fit the youth leader role. She saw everything in black and white.

Justin poured juice into the pitchers. He lifted his chin and smiled at Marcus. The idea that had rolled through his mind all night needed to come out. He just had to ask the guy and get it over with. Would Marcus laugh in his face?

He came up beside the giant. "Hey, do you have a minute?" The hotdogs needed time to cook, and all Justin needed was a moment of his time. Let the idea marinate. "I want to run an idea past you."

Marcus frowned.

Justin placed a hand on his shoulder. "Don't worry. I'm not going to ask you to lead a devotion or anything. I need a favor."

Marcus rolled some hotdogs, rested his utensils near the grill, and shrugged.

Justin waved Marcus to a cluster of trees out of earshot of Kyla. He scanned left and right, then leaned in. "This might sound a little crazy. You know how I mentioned I like a gal back in town."

Marcus gave a goofy grin. "Yeah."

"Her father is the sheriff, and he doesn't like me. He's got a thing against me for some stupid stuff I did when I was a teenager."

Marcus nodded and seemed to understand. No doubt he had gotten into mischief as a kid too.

"Don't take this the wrong way, but when I saw your tattoo, I got thinking how the sheriff would freak out if Leah dated someone with a tattoo like that."

Marcus widened his stance and crossed his arms. "What's this got to do with me? I don't want to date the sheriff's daughter." Marcus huffed.

Justin's face heated. "No." He swiped at his mouth and took a deep breath. "Like I said. This is going to sound crazy, but here goes." He swallowed hard. "What if you could go on a fake date with Leah? Meet her dad and—"

"—freak the sheriff out and make you look like the better choice." Marcus raked his fingers through his hair.

"Yeah." Justin gritted his teeth. "Something like that."

"What's in it for me?"

Justin dropped his arms to his sides. "I don't know. You can be our best man." He gave an awkward chuckle.

Marcus slapped his shoulder and belly laughed. From the trestle table, Kyla looked up and scowled, mouthing *shh.*

Justin gave him a sheepish smile. "What do you think?"

Marcus opened his mouth and paused for a moment. Perhaps it was for two seconds, but it seemed an eternity.

"Sure. I'll do it."

Sweet relief. Little chipmunks performed backflips in his belly. He couldn't wait to see the sheriff's face. Maybe he could strap a camera to Marcus. Nah, that was going too far, and the sheriff would arrest them both.

Marcus rubbed his palms. "I'm up for the challenge."

———

AFTER JUSTIN HAD INTRODUCED Leah to Chris and Marcus at the campsite, Chris suggested everyone take a trip to visit Leah's store and sample her products. Justin was the first to agree—any excuse to spend time with Leah.

As they stepped inside, the teen employee flinched. Justin didn't miss Nina pushing her phone behind the card machine, out of sight.

"Welcome to Trinity Organics." Leah waved the chefs inside.

"Fair dinkum." Marcus's mouth dropped open as his head turned, taking it all in. "This place is awesome." He turned to Chris and tugged on his sleeve. "We should expand the business and do something like this in Fremantle."

Chris chuckled. "It is impressive."

In the middle of the store, a haystack displayed baskets of produce of bright colors, all labeled with a chalkboard sign above showing the price. Green leeks, red rhubarb, and yellow peppers contributed to a nutritional rainbow.

The fridge shelving along the left wall held tubs of olives, sauerkraut, fermented foods, beans, frilly lettuce, and other greens.

On the right wall, rows of dispensers held cereals, nuts, grains of rice, and seeds. Brown paper bags and a weight scale sat on an old wine barrel.

Marcus beamed like a kid in a toy store. Leah enthusiastically pointed out each ingredient and explained their list of health benefits, including which ones were high in antioxidants. Marcus jumped in with personal accounts of various cooking techniques and recipes he had learned throughout his apprenticeship, and she looked impressed.

Marcus peeked inside a wooden box that had fresh herbs growing. He dramatically sniffed the air and moaned in delight. "Oh, what I could do with these."

Leah laughed and couldn't take her eyes off Marcus and his reactions to everything. The two seemed enthralled by their shared passion for food. Justin rubbed the back of his neck as they discussed intricate ingredient combinations. He was more comfortable talking about the properties of wood rather than food.

Marcus raised a finger in the air, facing Leah. "You should take me to the town's restaurants to sample the local cuisine sometime. We could be food critics for the night and write up a review for the local newspaper. That'll be good marketing for your store. Free press."

Leah lifted her palms. "Clever. I never thought of that."

Come on. It wasn't that clever. Justin could've come up with that idea.

The conversation progressed in the store until Chris suggested they go kayaking on the lake before they left town. Marcus and Leah were both excited at the suggestion.

Leah approached Nina. "Is that okay? Can you work another hour or two?"

Nina waved a hand. "For sure. I could do with the extra cash."

Justin held back a snort. The girl got paid for scrolling social media. The store was quiet today.

When they arrived at the rowing club on Lake Wainscott, it was like nothing Justin had ever seen before. The water was as blue as if the sky had fallen into the lake. The clear waters shimmered in the sunlight, and its banks lined with lush trees that swayed in the breeze. Trinity's biggest lake showcased its glory for the tourists today.

All four followed Hannah Gilbertson toward the dock in a line. They each wore the obligatory lifejackets, while Hannah hugged a bundle of paddles under her arm.

The sun heated the back of Justin's neck, and a bead of sweat trickled down his spine under the lifejacket.

Hannah stopped level with the three kayaks tied to buoys. "Sorry, most of our equipment is already rented out for the day.

But there's a double kayak, so you can all go." She handed out the paddles to each person and waved goodbye.

Marcus moved his bulky body into the double, amazingly not tipping the boat. He held out his hand to Leah and smiled.

What the–?

Leah took Marcus's hand and stepped into the two-person kayak.

Wait a minute. Justin's plan was to share the double with Leah and let Marcus and Chris take the singles. This wasn't turning out the way he'd envisioned. Leah was choosing Marcus over him. A tinge of jealousy wrapped around his throat as the fake couple pushed off into the water. Justin shook off his doubts. Leah and he had a strong connection, and that was why they were doing this in the first place. Marcus and Leah needed to get comfortable together to look like a real couple in front of her dad. Plus, Marcus would be gone in a couple of months.

Justin allowed Chris to go next, then settled into his kayak, gripping the plastic edge. The paddles were made of thin wood, and Justin guessed it was basswood under the laminate coating. He pushed away from the jetty's pillar and shielded his eyes from the glaring sun.

Marcus had paddled Leah halfway toward the bridge already. How did the guy do that? Superhuman strength, no doubt. Justin worked his shoulders to catch up the best he could. Good thing Leah wasn't the type to compare him to Marcus, as Justin would lose on every front. Marcus had it all— talented chef, enthusiastic about organic food, bulging biceps, Australian accent, good looking, funny. It was enough to make anyone feel sick.

Was the swirling in his gut the water, or the idea of Leah falling for Marcus for real? That wouldn't happen. "No way. Not Leah."

Despite his words, the unease in his body stayed with him for the rest of the day.

CHAPTER SIX

The doorbell rang, and Leah pressed her hands to her stomach. "That must be him." She smiled at Dad. "Now, make sure you're nice, and don't interrogate him. He's not one of your suspects."

"I'm not a lawyer, baby girl."

"I know that, but you do like to be thorough."

"I appreciate how you've listened to my advice, and I'm honored that you invited him over to meet me first. I can't wait to interroga—chat with him." He winked and waved his fingers. "Go answer the door."

Leah nibbled on her bottom lip. Had she done the right thing? She hustled to the front room, flung open the door, and sucked in a breath at the sight of Marcus filling the doorway. The guy had looked huge next to Justin, but he towered over her. He'd need to tuck his head to get into the house. He must eat whole chickens for lunch every day or something crazy. Justin had mentioned he was some kind of heavyweight champion.

"Welcome to our humble home." She gritted out a smile and whispered between her teeth. "Thanks for doing this."

"No worries. This will make my trip to America more memorable. Anyway, I like your man."

Leah put a finger to her lips. "He's not my man yet. He will be after our little plan has been executed." Leah stood back and waved him inside and led him to the kitchen-dining area.

Heavy footsteps followed her. The wooden flooring underneath the carpet creaked under his weight. He was like the Incredible Hulk without green skin. How would Dad react when he discovered Marcus's tattoo? Dad had quoted the Old Testament when she was younger. She'd never get a tattoo anyway. For all she knew, the ink chemicals could seep into her system and do who knew what. Skin was the largest organ of the body. Second, she hated needles. No one could pay her to go through that amount of pain or discomfort. She'd rather buy a T-shirt with a meaningful message. At least she could change her mind and switch out the shirt whenever she wanted.

Mom noticed Marcus first. Her eyes went so wide, she might burst a retinal artery. Dad glanced from the dining table and blinked but quickly hid his shock. He stood and pushed back his chair.

"Hi. You must be Marcus." Dad came around the table and shook Marcus's hand. From Dad's expression, Marcus must've squeezed hard.

Oh dear.

Dad's face screwed into a weird expression she'd never seen before, a mix between fear and anger. Maybe anger for how Marcus had crushed his hand and fear that Leah would date him. That must be it.

Mom cleared her throat. "Dinner's ready. Please, everyone, have a seat." Mom had already positioned the dinner rolls at the center of the table, along with a butter dish and knife. She brought two bowls of soup at a time and placed them before each place setting.

Leah took the spot opposite Marcus. He gave her a mischievous grin. What was going on in that head of his? His expression suggested he had a wicked plan going on.

"This is for starters, and we have a main course and dessert."

"Smells great. I love my food." Marcus grinned.

Dad flicked a cloth napkin over his lap. "Leah tells me you're a professional cook."

"Yes. I am a qualified chef."

"And by your accent, you're an Australian."

Marcus looked at Leah. "Honey, you didn't tell him?"

Her eyes went wide. Calling her honey was going too far—it sounded like they were already dating. Dad quirked a brow at Leah and frowned at Marcus. "Do you live around here, or are you on vacation?"

"I've come to help at the summer camp. My boss used to volunteer at the camps when he lived in the States. He convinced me that a working holiday would be a great experience. So I'm here, touring and working." He gave Leah a goofy grin. "Maybe find love, then head back to Australia."

Dad's lips dropped into a thin line, turning in and out like he was chewing on brittle sand.

Mom's lashes flitted like she had a stuck eyelash. "Well, that's quite an interesting …" She scratched her chin. "An interesting goal, I guess you'd call it."

Marcus nodded. "Yep. I'm a man on a mission. When I see what I want, I get what I want. Nothing stands in my way." He stared at Leah with a hungry look in his eyes.

Leah gulped hard. Justin had employed the perfect actor. Even she was almost convinced.

Dad's face turned from white to pink to red to gray and back to his usual color. A lot of mixed emotions must be going on in his mind right now. An awkward silence descended in the room. How could she save this situation? Dad was freaking out.

But why would she save the situation? This was what she and Justin wanted. It was going perfectly to plan.

Leah took a deep breath. "I'd love to visit Australia. It sounds like a beautiful place. Doesn't it, Mom? We've always wanted to go."

Mom shook her head violently. "I didn't say I wanted to go to Australia."

"Yeah, Mom, I think you did. You said you wanted to cuddle the koalas."

Marcus chuckled. "Koalas aren't that cuddly. They've got sharp claws and are likely to pee on you. And they smell funny. But they're nice to look at through the bars at the zoo. I haven't seen them anywhere else. We have lots of kangaroos." He patted his belly. "They make a nice burger. All organic. Very healthy."

Mom snapped her head backward causing possible whiplash. "You eat them?"

"Yeah. Americans eat deer, don't they?"

"Some do." Mom blinked, dipped her spoon into her soup, and took a sip. Her gaze darted toward her husband and back to Marcus just as he winked at Leah. He should stop that. Dad might catch on. He was a smart cop.

Leah shifted in her seat. "I hear some places in Australia are right into organics. It would be a great place to open an organic shop, don't you think, Marcus?"

He took a slow slurp of his soup, making a ridiculously loud noise. A dribble of pumpkin soup trickled down his chin. Was he doing it on purpose? Or was he a sloppy pig in real life?

"Where I come from, there are lots of hippies, vegans, and people worried about the environment. You'd fit right in, Leah. You need to come and see it for yourself. You can stay at my place by the beach."

Dad's elbow slammed into the table, and everyone looked in his direction. Dad was usually a man of self-control. "Excuse me," he said in a weird voice that sounded like a tortured moose. His words wobbled and came out deeper than usual.

Mom put her hand on dad's arm and looked at Marcus. "We've raised our daughter to high standards, so she wouldn't be staying at a young man's house. She would need to be chaperoned."

Marcus rocked back in his chair and let out a belly laugh. "She's twenty-four and she needs a chaperone. What kind of religion is this?"

Dad placed his palm on the table with a surprising measure of control. "Do you have any religious beliefs, Marcus?"

"My boss is a Christian. He wants me converted or something. I think that's why he came up with this summer camp idea. Look, I believe in God, for sure. He made the world. It's flipping obvious. But yeah, let's just say I'm not walking in the ways of the Lord." He used air quotes. "I'm not convinced about the not sleeping together before marriage thing or not getting drunk. I'm more liberated than living to strict rules."

Mom smothered a gasp with her hand. Once Marcus had left their house, Leah was in for a long lecture.

————

"WHAT IN THE world do you think you were doing, bringing that kind of man into our home?" Dad's jugular veins looked about to pop out of his neck.

Leah put a finger to her lips. "Marcus is probably still walking down the garden path. He might hear you."

"I don't care if he hears me. He's not coming back here."

"Dad, you haven't given him a chance. Sure, he's not strong in his faith yet, but he's a nice guy. You wanted me to date other men and not 'settle' for Justin because he's the first man who's ever liked me."

Dad fisted his hips. "Justin isn't the first man who has liked you."

Leah crossed her arms. "What do you mean by that statement?"

"Others have looked at you in that way. But they see me behind you or beside you." Dad lifted his chin. "They know they don't live up to my standards."

"So that's why no one from Trinity Lakes has ever bothered to date me—because they know they're not high and mighty enough for your approval. That basically means I can only date tourists."

"Excuse me, young lady. I don't like the tone of your voice."

Dad was usually a softy, but when he put his foot down, there was no way of changing his mind. That was the root of his problem with Justin—his attitude. Justin apparently wasn't good enough for her.

"Dad, Marcus is going to summer camp and will hear life-transforming messages. We need to have grace and not judge. You know what the Bible says. We can't be hypocrites."

Dad turned and strode away. He did that when he knew he might say something he'd likely regret. He couldn't argue with her statement. Dad knew the Bible better than her and must realize he'd judged Marcus based on his outward appearance and apparent ignorance. Sure, Marcus was rough around the edges. But he was playing it up deliberately. Justin looked like an absolute saint in comparison, which was what Justin wanted.

Leah followed her father into the living area. "Can we talk this through? You asked me to date other men, and Marcus coming to dinner is what dating other men looks like—me getting to know them as a person. And I included you and Mom." She swung her hands behind her back. "I like Marcus. I want to spend more time with him while he's here in the States."

Dad flopped into his favorite leather recliner. "You don't seriously want to move to Australia. You spoke like you'd consider selling your business after all the work you put into it. How could you start in a strange country you know nothing about?"

"I have Australian friends. There are a bunch of them in Trinity Lakes. It sounds like a wonderful place to raise a family. And maybe I wouldn't have to move to Australia. Marcus could stay here. This town could do with another good restaurant."

Dad crossed his arms over his chest. "I can't believe we're having this conversation. You don't even know the guy, and you're talking about marriage and moving to Australia." Dad slapped his forehead. "Correction. Not marriage because Marcus doesn't believe in the rules. He believes you can sleep around, and God's okay with that."

"Dad, that's not what he said. Anyhow, I wouldn't marry him unless he had the same convictions as I do. I'm not throwing away my beliefs because some guy with muscles charms me."

Dad pointed and waggled his finger. "See, you just like him for his …" Dad flapped his hand around. "… his bulging biceps."

Leah burst out laughing but stopped mid-cackle when dad's lips flatlined. This was not funny. Not for him. Maybe she had taken this a little too far. "All right, Dad. How about we let it go tonight? I will be a welcoming member of the community and show Marcus some of the sights of Trinity Lakes."

Dad shook his head. "I don't want you spending time with him alone. That's not a good idea."

"Dad, I know what I'm doing. I'll ensure we're in public and accountable to my community. Nothing intimate is going to happen between Marcus and me."

Dad's eyes went wide. "You better believe nothing intimate is happening between you and that neck-tattooed hooligan."

"But Daddy, it was your idea." Leah made sure she sounded innocent, but not so innocent that Dad would realize he was being played.

"I was thinking of some nice guy from church. Not an uneducated heathen who looks like he'd be more at home in prison."

"Justin Perry is a nice guy from church."

Dad frowned.

Leah held up her hand. "All right. We better let this go for now. I can tell you're upset."

"I'm agitated, and I need to calm down. We'll talk about this another time."

CHAPTER SEVEN

Justin stood in the center of the workshop, surrounded by the low hum of machinery and the smell of freshly cut wood. He had spent the morning crafting a new display cabinet for one client and was now ready to cut a perfect angle for his next job—period bathroom cabinets for the renovation at the Lakeview Inn.

Taking a deep breath, he bent at the waist and lowered the miter saw into the plank of wood. Sawdust sprayed from either side as the machine vibrated in his hands, yet Justin remained focused, guiding the blade with precision. He clicked off the power, slid his safety glasses to the top of his head, and blew the sawdust away. Perfect cut.

A yard away, Billy waved a hand, gaining his attention. Justin removed his earmuffs. "What's up?"

"Leah is here to see you." Billy waggled his brows.

Justin jolted upright and banged his head into a wooden shelf above him. He rubbed at the back of his head. Why did he always get clumsy around Leah? Just her name made his heart jump in his chest. He wiped his sweaty palms on his overalls and assessed his grubby appearance. It wasn't like she hadn't seen him like this before. But he scrubbed up okay for church or around town.

Leah stood behind the yellow safety line painted on the concrete floor. Her face lit up with her broad smile when they locked eyes. The woman must have the whitest teeth in all of Trinity Lakes. She didn't drink coffee or tea, unless it was green tea. Yuck.

His strides increased as he came toward her. He would love to run and whisk her into his arms and swing Leah around. That was how she made him feel inside. How would she react if he did something like that? One day, he would be able to twirl her around, making her laugh. He loved that laugh.

"Hey, beautiful. What makes you wanna visit my grubby workshop, which is unsuitable for a princess?"

She waved a hand down. "Hey, I'm okay with getting my hands dirty. I enjoy gardening and hard work."

"I didn't say that you weren't hard-working. You are. You've done an amazing job with getting your business started."

"Thank you. But that's not what I'm here to talk about." Leah swung her arms behind her back. "I've got to be quick. I put a sign on the shop door that I'll be back in ten minutes."

Justin shoved his hands in his overall pockets. "Shoot away. What's going on?"

"Have you spoken to Marcus?"

"Yes, he gave me the rundown of what happened last night after he left your place. Sounds like it went well."

Leah looked to the ceiling and shook her head, but a sly grin grew up her cheeks. "I wish I had filmed it, Justin. You should've seen Dad's face. He totally freaked out. He thinks I might sell my business and move to Australia. And get this—he actually thinks I would live with Marcus. Unmarried."

Justin laughed. "Wow, that would freak him out. Even the idea is freaking me out."

"I would never do anything like that. You know me—always following the rules."

"It's not about following the rules. You believe it and you live it. It's something you want to do. No one's forcing you."

"That's true." She scuffed her sneaker over the polished concrete. "Look, Justin. I don't know if Dad will change his mind even if he's comparing you to Marcus. And now Dad doesn't want me to have anything to do with Marcus. When I said I wanted to be a friend and show him around town, Dad couldn't finish the conversation."

"Woah. The sheriff lost for words? Amazing."

Machinery buzzed and echoed around the warehouse. Justin touched Leah's elbow and led her toward the exit. He couldn't hear properly over the noise, and he needed to get back to work. He let go of her elbow and smiled at her. "So the night was a good start, anyhow."

"Marcus acted up for the part and seemed to enjoy every minute. He's an outsider, so he's not scared of Dad like the rest of Trinity Lakes'. Marcus thinks he can do what he likes as long as he doesn't break the law."

"Yeah, but let's not get him deported."

"So what do we do now?"

"You need to go on another date."

"With Marcus?" Leah shook her hands in a no-no-no gesture. "Dad doesn't want me to."

"But you said you were going to show him around town. Why don't you?"

"I did say that." Her brow creased in cute concentration. He had the urge to smooth out the wrinkle on her forehead and tell her not to stress.

"I'd only be out with him in the public eye. Nothing inappropriate would happen."

"Of course. Why don't you go on a picnic by the lake? Pretend you're really into Marcus. Word will get back to your dad that you're out with a rough-looking guy. Then your dad will get more nervous.'"

She lifted her palms. "If that's what you want. Do you think it'll work?"

"He still needs to accept me. This is one way of pushing the process a little faster." He hooked his pinky finger with hers and swung her arm. "Because I don't want to wait seven years." It had already been five years of liking her.

Leah's cheeks flushed pink. "It's not going to take seven years."

"No. I don't want another seven more days without you. Seven minutes." He stepped closer, and the desire to kiss her grew stronger. "Or seven seconds. I just want to be with you, walking hand in hand around Trinity Lakes, not worrying what people say or think."

She looked up at him through her lashes. "You're so sweet, Justin." She swung his arm three times and let go. "All right. I must go. Get Marcus to call me, and we'll set up this picnic date."

———

LEAH FOLLOWED Marcus toward Lake Wainscott as he held a picnic basket in one hand and a rolled-up blanket under his arm. The sun's light glinted off the lake's surface like diamonds, dancing in the surrounding trees, creating a breathtaking picture.

She pointed to a patch of grass that lay between a cluster of trees and the sandbank. "How about there?" People would be able to see them but also think they were trying to have some privacy.

Marcus turned over his shoulder. "Sure." He got to work and smoothed out the red and white checkered blanket.

Leah stood with nothing to do but watch. This kind of felt

like an actual date. She hadn't been on many. Could she count the trip to the state zoo with Alex? His little nephew came along, so maybe not.

Past a few trees on the left, children giggled at the playground. Was that Melanie's sister pushing her son on a swing? Oh boy. It was getting real now. People would soon assume Leah was dating Marcus. How could Justin think this was a good idea?

"Is everything okay?" Marcus studied her face.

"I'm a little nervous. Sure, it's a fake date, but I don't know how to act. I don't even know you that well."

Marcus removed his jacket. "That's the purpose of dating. We're getting to know each other, right?" He laughed. "Relax. I might have a neck tattoo, but I'm not that scary." He winked. "I'm just a cuddly teddy bear. Promise." He patted his belly that showed he liked food.

Marcus was fun. She had nothing to worry about.

"When did you get your tattoo?" Leah sat and tucked her feet under her thighs.

"It does look professional, but an amateur did it. My friend from high school is a talented artist. He dreamed of becoming a tattooist, and a bunch of us volunteered to be his guinea pigs. I was the sixth person he had worked on, so he tattooed like a pro by the time he got to me." He kneeled and removed a disposable bamboo container from the cane basket. "I do regret it, though. Thankfully my chef's uniform covers most of it."

"I've heard about eighty percent of young people regret their tattoo after a few years. I couldn't do it. It must be painful."

"Can't remember. I was drunk at the time."

"Oh, right." Leah pushed up to kneel next to him and peered into the basket. "What's on the menu?"

"I have the most amazing lunch prepared, even if I do say so myself. Sit back and let me serve you."

Leah leaned back and ensured her long skirt covered her legs. Marcus removed two glasses and a bottle of wine.

"I don't drink wine. My dad's very strict. We've never had alcohol in the house. As a police officer, I guess he's seen a lot of what alcoholism can do, so he didn't want any available."

"I've grown out of the reckless phase, so I don't get drunk anymore. I was exaggerating to your dad about all that stuff. But I'm a chef. It's my job to know how to pair up a fruity Shiraz or a red to accentuate the flavors of a meal. And I do appreciate a nice wine with certain meals."

Leah nodded. He knew a lot about food, that was for sure.

Marcus removed a container of mixed blueberries, fresh raspberries, and grapes. He arranged the fruit on a platter, along with freshly cut watermelon.

He took out two bottles—orange juice and something Leah didn't recognize.

"I bought juice, or you might want to try this organic cider. I was stoked when I found it was available here. It's a well-known brand from Margaret River, a famous surfing spot in Western Australia. I love to travel down there on my breaks."

"You surf?"

"Occasionally."

Leah inched forward and plucked a blueberry before squishing it between her back teeth. A burst of flavor ignited her taste buds. "These are so much better fresh than frozen. I haven't been able to source fresh organic ones here."

"Sorry, but the berries aren't organic. The cider is. Everything else I picked from the local market."

She waved a hand. "It's fine. Thanks for going to so much effort, Marcus. For a fake date, you've done exceptionally well. Imagine what you'd be like on a real one."

He guffawed. "I'm not much of a romantic. But I am passionate about food." Marcus repositioned some savory crackers and cheese. "What would you like to drink?"

"The cider, of course. If it's good, I might stock it in my shop."

"Where do you get your supplies from?" Marcus opened the bottle and poured her a glass.

"Mostly from wholesalers in Walla Walla. They have crates and crates of quality produce. I place my orders on Sunday and Wednesday nights, and it's packed the next day. If there's a local going to Walla Walla, they'll pick it up for me in exchange for a mixed fruit and vegetable box. Otherwise, it's delivered first thing in the morning."

Marcus passed her the drink and leaned on his elbow, head in his palm, peering up at her with interest.

"The dried goods come in via a courier company."

Marcus popped a grape into his mouth. "These aren't bad."

Leah took a small sip of the cider. The sour liquid bubbled over her tongue. "This is quite refreshing."

"Yep. Our local produce is something else. Margaret River has a lot of restaurants and vineyards. I would move down there, but I like working for Chris in the city."

"How did you meet him? Were you his apprentice?"

Marcus looked out to the lake. The surrounding trees mirrored on the surface. "I struggled as a young person and joined a youth program managed by Chris's wife. They weren't married at the time, though. Chris mentored young men, and he offered some of us an apprenticeship when we graduated from the program. It wasn't long before I was winning young chef awards."

"Wow. That's awesome."

"I'm very thankful. That's why I said yes when Chris asked me to help him with summer camp. I wasn't keen at first, but it's hard to say no to the man who has changed your life."

"That's sweet." Leah took another sip of cider.

"I don't know if I'd call it sweet, but it's nice to have a good mate like Chris. Someone to look up to. He keeps me on the straight and narrow."

Leah's heart warmed. Or was the cider giving her heartburn?

"I work six to seven days a week. That's why Chris convinced me to have a working holiday. It's hard for me to take time off from work. I like to keep busy."

"I can relate." Leah grinned. "When you own your own business, it sometimes becomes all-consuming."

Marcus sat upright and opened his bottle of wine. "This will balance out the sharp-tasting cheese."

Leah drained her glass. "I'll stick with the cider, thanks." She poured herself a glass with a *glug, glug, glug.*

Marcus quirked a brow. Was she doing it wrong? Or should she have let him pour the drink? He wasn't her waiter, and this was a fake date.

"Don't forget I brought orange juice too—if you prefer."

"No, this is delicious. I'm super thirsty."

He shrugged and plated up a selection of fruits, cheeses, and meats. He added a bamboo fork and slid it across to her. "Bon Appetit."

She giggled. "Shouldn't you use an Australian phrase?"

"Go on, cobber. Get that grub into ya." He exaggerated his accent.

Cider sprayed from her mouth and dribbled down her chin. She slapped a hand to her mouth. Oh, what a dork.

Marcus burst out laughing and swiped at his denim jeans. "I wasn't expecting that reaction."

"I'm so sorry." She plucked a paper napkin and dabbed at his knee. Leah lost her balance, tilted sideways, and her backside thumped to the ground. Something hard jabbed into her thigh under the blanket. Must be a rock or a tree root.

Marcus shook his head, grinning, and took the napkin from her, then wiped his pants. What a class act she was. Fortunately, he seemed amused by her clumsiness. Good thing she wasn't trying to impress him.

A family walked along the shoreline of the lake.

"Hopefully more people will come and see us," she said.

"Yeah. Let's link arms to make a toast."

"Okay." She leaned forward, and they crossed arms while holding their drinks. "What do we toast to?"

"To you and Justin. May you become a couple soon. And may you pay for my flights back to the US to be the best man."

"Ha ha. We will owe you one." They sipped their drinks, smiling at each other. Marcus was a nice guy, and it was easy to relax around him. It was sweet that he wanted the best for her and Justin and was willing to play along to help.

She unlinked her arm from his and finished her drink. The flavor seemed to have a hint of apple. "I'm a big fan of kombucha. This tastes just like it, but more apple."

"Yes, it's basically fermented apple juice." Marcus swirled his glass and took two gulps of his red wine.

He could drink red wine like water, and it had no noticeable effect on him. She wasn't big, and she wasn't used to alcohol. One glass of his wine would probably make her tipsy. She'd play it safe and stick with the organic cider. "What else do we have in this picnic basket?"

Marcus held up a finger. "You will not be disappointed. I managed to cook up some delicious Mediterranean vegetables and added them to a chicken wrap."

"Yum."

"But first, try some of the cheeses." He used a knife to slice some off a block. "This one is sharp and crumbly. Perfect on a cracker." He smoothed the sliver onto a cracker and handed it to her. "Goes nicely with the cider too."

Leah glanced at her empty glass. "Looks like I need a refill."

"You've finished two glasses already? That was quick. You

are thirsty. I should have a bottle of spring water in here some-where." He rummaged in the basket.

"There's plenty of cider left."

He frowned at her. "I thought you didn't drink much."

"They're small glasses. As I said, I'm thirsty today." She flapped her hand to her cheeks. "We're not even in the direct sun, and I'm burning up. It's a hot day." Leah grabbed the bottle of cider, filled her glass, and held it to the light. Tiny bubbles floated to the top. She brought her glass to her lips and took a long sip. It sure did cleanse the palette.

After ten minutes of chatting about Australia and discovering more about Marcus, she devoured her chicken wrap. Her belly became bloated, and the temptation to fall asleep tugged at her. A little nap sounded amazing right now.

But first, she needed to wet her tongue. Her mouth felt like cotton balls. She reached for the last of the organic cider, but Marcus held her wrist. "I don't think that's a good idea. You shouldn't be drinking during the day."

"What are you talking about? It's cider."

"Still, you shouldn't have too much."

"It doesn't have any alcohol in it, does it?"

"Of course it does. Not a lot—maybe the same amount as beer—but it's definitely got alcohol."

"But cider doesn't have alcohol."

"Australian cider does. Maybe you have a different word for it in the US. It's certified organic, but it does contain alcohol. Look." Marcus collected the bottle and showed her the ingredients.

There it was in black and white. Leah covered her mouth. "No wonder I'm feeling woozy and sleepy."

"Sorry. Now it makes sense. I thought you were drinking because you're not allowed to drink at your parent's house." He slapped a palm to his forehead. "Justin is going to kill me."

Leah shook her head. And that was a stupid move. Now her

vision swam as if she'd been on one of those spinning rides at the playground. "Justin will understand. It's only a silly miscommunication." She pressed the back of her hand to her forehead. "Any other person would be fine. I'm just not used to alcohol."

Marcus stretched his body out over the picnic blanket, rubbing his head, looking to the sky. "I'm an idiot."

This was getting uncomfortable. She brushed the remaining crumbs from her skirt. "We should go now." Leah stood, but her left knee bent inward. She stumbled and tripped over Marcus's third leg. Three legs?

His palms shot up to stop her from crashing into him, but it didn't work. She fell across his torso and stared into his face. His very shocked face.

Leah burst out laughing, and spit flew from her mouth. "Oh my goodness." She gasped before swiping her germs from his face. "Oops." She laughed again.

Marcus blinked his surprise. His large hands rested on her waist, and his grin grew wide. "It's not every day a pretty woman spits in my face."

A strand of her hair fell into his eyes, and she giggled. "I'm such a klutz." He looked blurry. "The world is spinning a little bit."

Twigs snapped nearby and leaves rustled. Both Marcus and Leah jerked their gazes to the bushes where pink and purple clothing peeked amongst the trees.

Leah pushed up from Marcus's chest. "Someone's spying on us."

"That's what we want, isn't it? To be noticed?"

She glanced down at him. Her eyes went wide at what this must look like. Leah commando rolled onto her back. She knocked a wine bottle over, and it spilled its contents onto the grass.

Fan-freaking-tastic.

She faced the big blue sky. The clouds moved way too fast.

And in circles—how weird. Leah pointed heavenward. "Don't tell me this is the apocalypse. This is not good timing if it is."

"Huh?" Marcus's voice seemed like he was miles away. His voice echoed again, "Leah, Leah. Are you okay?"

"Yeah." She moaned. "Just give me a few minutes. I think I'll lie down here for a bit."

"You do that. Close your eyes, and I'll pack up everything. We don't want you tripping over anything."

His gentle chuckle lulled her to sleep.

CHAPTER EIGHT

Rhonda Ingalls burst into Justin's workshop, placed her hand to her chest, heaving as though she'd run around the lake three times over.

"Rhonda, what's wrong?" Justin rushed toward her and placed a hand on her shoulder. "Are you having an asthma attack?"

She straightened and flapped her hand, huffing. "No. I had to come straight away. You need to know."

Panic rippled through him. Had someone been hurt? One of the youth?

"Leah was making out with a tourist." Her eyes went wide. "At the lake. In front of everyone."

Justin shifted on his feet. The words stung, but in context, Leah and Marcus must be playing it up for their audience.

"Calm down, Rhonda. You must have your story wrong. Leah doesn't go around kissing strangers."

"I know you're in love with her. I see the way you look at Leah. That's why you needed to know first. Go find her and tell her she's making a huge mistake."

Justin scratched his head. "Leah and I are friends. That's all.

If she wants to date other guys, I can't stop her." Anyhow, this was all fake. How perfect that the town gossip saw them. Everything was going according to plan.

Rhonda propped her hands on her hips. "Justin. Leah is being taken advantage of. She's an innocent young lady. That man got her drunk and is taking advantage of her."

"Drunk?" Not his Leah. She had never had a sip of alcohol in her life. Her father wouldn't allow it.

"Yes. They were rolling around on top of each other, laughing. And there was an empty wine bottle beside the picnic blanket."

An atomic bomb exploded in his chest. He jolted back from Rhonda. "Are you sure?" He barely managed to get the words out.

"Positive."

He ran a hand down his cheek, tugging at his skin. Purity was one of the many things he found attractive in Leah. but maybe her morals were about pleasing her dad. Perhaps she'd be more liberal if she had the choice. She knew about Justin's alcoholic dad and why he chose to stay away from the stuff. He needed a partner who supported his decisions.

Right now, Justin needed space. He'd wait for Leah to explain, but first, he needed to calm down. Maybe she wasn't the one for him. Would she continue to date Marcus if he backed off? If Leah were the one for Justin, she would choose him over Marcus.

"I need to get back to work." He spun to leave.

"Justin. You can't let her get away with this. And you can't let that hoodlum of a man take advantage of her."

Justin snapped to face Rhonda. "Then why didn't you do anything to stop them?"

Her face flushed red. "I didn't want to look like I was snooping. And I wasn't. Anyhow, it's not my place to save her. You should be the hero."

"Pfft. I'm not her hero. Obviously. I'm easily replaced."

Rhonda gave an exasperated sigh. "I'm disappointed in you, young man. I didn't want to tell the sheriff, but if you won't do anything, I'll need to find her father."

Justin shrugged and strode away as if it didn't matter to him. But he secretly hoped the sheriff would twist Marcus's arm and shove him into a tree trunk. Hard.

———

MARCUS GENTLY TOUCHED Leah's shoulder. "Wake up, sleeping beauty."

Leah blinked, her vision still swimming. "How long have I been asleep?"

"About twenty minutes. Are you feeling better?" Marcus knelt beside her. "Can you make it to the car park?"

"Huh?" Her voice sounded a mile away to her own ears.

"The parking lot."

She rolled to her side and tried to focus on Marcus. "Will you drive?"

"I'm going to have to. I can't believe you got tipsy from a few small glasses. It would take me six glasses to have the tiniest effect. But I guess I'm twice your body weight."

"My house isn't far. Have you driven in the States before?"

"No, but how hard can it be to drive on the other side of the road?"

She couldn't think, and there was no way she could drive. Hold on. She couldn't go back to her house. What if Mom noticed she was tipsy? "Can you drop me off at a friend's house? Then come back later when I've slept this off and take me home."

"Sure." Marcus held out a hand. "Let's get this drunken princess to a secret castle."

Leah kneaded her palm into her eye socket. The movement

didn't clear her fuzzy vision or her muddled brain. "Don't say that. It sounds terrible." She slipped her hand into his.

"Sorry. I won't bring it up again." He carefully helped her to stand. "And please don't bring up your lunch."

She steadied herself, but her body swayed and crashed into his chest. He held her upright.

"Leah Maranatha Thompson!" Her father bellowed from behind her. "What do you think you're doing?"

Marcus jumped back, and Leah stumbled without his support.

Dressed in his sheriff's uniform, Dad stormed over and grabbed her by the wrist. "You've been drinking."

Leah wobbled. "I didn't know it was alcohol."

"You spiked my daughter's drink?" Dad snarled at Marcus.

He held up his palms. "No, sir. She only had a couple of glasses. She didn't realize, and I assumed—"

Dad waggled his finger in Marcus's face, even though the giant overpowered Dad in height and stature. "Stay away from Leah."

She tugged her arm free. "Dad, Marcus did nothing wrong. It was a misunderstanding."

Dad turned to face her. "I'm very disappointed in you."

"I can see that." Leah hiccupped, then gave a dopey smile.

Marcus's lips turned upward on one side before he wiped his mouth with his palm, doing a terrible job of keeping a straight face. He wasn't the one getting busted.

Hold on. How old was she? Twenty-four. Who did Dad think he was, scolding her in front of her date? Fake date, but still totally embarrassing.

"You're coming home with me." Dad's voice held no room for negotiation.

"No. I'm not a little girl anymore." Leah hugged herself. "You don't get to boss me around."

"The house rules haven't changed. No drinking, no drugs, and go to church on Sundays. I'm going to breathalyze you."

"Dad. Are you not hearing me? I'm an adult. You don't get to control me." She dropped her arms to her sides, stretching and clenching her fingers. "This is why men avoid me—because you're overbearing and watch my every move." She hooked her arm around Marcus's. "The only person willing to date me is a foreigner who doesn't know my sad situation."

Marcus frowned and patted her hand. "I'm sure lots of guys would want to go out with you."

She shook her head. "No. They're scared of him." She pointed at her father and then stared at Marcus. "You're the only brave one." If only Justin would have stood up to Dad instead of coming up with this stupid plan. He should've made an effort to get to know her father if he truly wanted to become a part of the family.

Dad waved a hand up and down in Marcus's direction. "This is the kind of person you want to spend your time with?"

A flush of heat filled her cheeks. "Don't talk about my friends like that. You've gone too far this time." Leah gripped Marcus's arm tighter, using him for the strength she didn't have. Strength to tell her father what she really thought. "No more, Dad. You need to leave."

"I will. And so can you. You, young lady, can pack your bags and have your things gone before I get home tonight." His voice rose a million decibels, thudding into her skull. "That is an order!" Dad turned on his heel and strode toward his vehicle.

Marcus rubbed her hand. "Crikey. He is one angry bull ant."

"Bull is the keyword. He's trying to bully me into not associating with you." She faced him. "He's kicking me out of the family home."

"It's probably time you moved out anyway. Like you said, he's controlling."

Leah stepped away from Marcus and rubbed her swirling stomach. Her insides swished with a nervous mixture of uncertainty and doubt. "I guess it's time. My business is doing well. I've nearly paid off my loan." She stared out toward the sparkling lake. "I can afford to move out. I don't know why I haven't." She smiled at him and shrugged. "Looks like today is the day."

He gave a small chuckle. "Yep. Where will you go?"

"I could stay with my best friend, if her husband doesn't mind. She just got married." Her eyes lit up. "I should introduce you to Adam. He's an Aussie and is into fitness too. Do you know him?"

"Probably not, but I'd love to meet him."

LEAH, Marcus, Melanie, and Adam sat around the dining table, all a little lost for words.

"That sucks." Melanie finally broke the silence.

"Did he really mean it?" Adam's tone signaled his disbelief.

"Too bad if he didn't. I'm leaving anyway." Now she just had to find somewhere to go.

Adam ran a hand through his hair. "Where are you going to live?" Another awkward silence passed through the group.

Melanie glared at Adam with a look that contained a whole conversation. Her eyes widened, then narrowed. Adam glanced at Leah, then back at his wife. A frown creased his forehead.

Melanie rolled her eyes and huffed.

"Ouch." Adam jerked to the side and rubbed at something under the table. He tilted his head toward his wife, then straightened in his chair. "We have a spare bedroom at the back of the house. You'll have some privacy but share our kitchen."

Leah darted a glance between the newlywed couple. This wasn't "Plan A" for them or her, either. "I wouldn't want to impose. You've only been married for a few months."

Melanie waved a hand. "Feels like a century."

Adam's mouth twisted to one side.

"The best century of my life." Melanie squeezed his hand.

His face seemed to relax, and that lovesick puppy dog expression he usually wore around Melanie returned.

"Aw. You guys are awesome together. The sweetest couple I know." A longing expanded in Leah's chest. Who would make her feel that lovestruck? "Okay, I'll stay for a week or so while I find a place to rent. Maybe someone has a studio apartment available. I don't need much space."

Melanie patted the back of Leah's hand. "You stay as long as you need to, babe. We've got your back."

Leah's eyelids burned. She'd told her dad that she wasn't a little girl anymore. She was moving out. Moving on.

It was time to do the whole adulting thing.

———

AN HOUR LATER, Leah had her best friend by her side to face Mom. Had Mom heard the news yet? Leah pushed open the unlocked door but didn't call out as usual.

Adam had taken Marcus to the gym at the country club, where they'd wait for the call from Melanie when Leah's things were packed.

Melanie followed behind her, holding the flattened boxes Adam had used when he shipped his belongings from Australia.

"Is that you, Leah?" Mom called from the direction of the kitchen.

Leah glanced over her shoulder at her friend. "Here goes nothing. Don't let me collapse in a heap, sobbing on Mom's shoulder."

"You can do this." Melanie nodded. "Big girl panties."

Leah laughed. This was why they got along so well. Melanie was a force to be reckoned with as a marketing guru. She moved forward, never looking back. Melanie was a few years older and had more life experience. But they'd clicked over their shared interest in health and pure foods the first day Melanie walked into Trinity Organics.

The hallway opened to the bright kitchen. Old fashioned awnings framed the window overlooking the veranda out the back. Mom spun around, lowering a mug from the top cabinet. "Just in time for a coffee." She blinked at Melanie. "Oh, hi." Mom frowned at the cardboard boxes. "You two look like you're on a mission. What're your plans for the day?" Mom pressed the button on the percolator.

"Dad hasn't called you?"

Mom tucked away curly strands of hair from her cheek. "Should he have?"

Leah mounted a breakfast bar stool and leaned her elbows on the counter. "Dad barged in on my picnic date with Marcus. Dad told me not to associate with him anymore."

Mom tapped her chin. "I feel like there's more to the story."

She squirmed and mentally tugged her big girl panties into place. She forced a laugh. "Funny story. Did you know Australian cider has alcohol? Well, I didn't. I thought I was drinking good ol' American sparkling cider—"

Melanie slashed her hand through the air and her face bore the message, *get to the point.*

LEAH DREW in a breath and squared her shoulders. "I was dru—" Heat rose her chest. She couldn't even say it. "Woozy."

Mom huffed. "Seriously, Leah. Do you like this Australian man?" Mom glanced at Melanie. "Not that there's anything wrong with Australian men. I mean, the accent and all." Mom fanned herself. "But Marcus." Her brows knitted together. "I didn't see you liking that kind of guy."

Leah's feet went hot like she'd walked through a campfire

with the same annoyance she'd experienced with Dad. Burning anger traveled all through her body. Her parents were overprotective, controlling, and too judgmental, all because Marcus had a tattoo he regretted getting as a teenager. Sure, he had terrible table manners, but he seemed genuine. His rawness and rough edges were refreshing compared to some Christians she knew, the kind who wore masks and pretended everything was okay.

Ooh. Was she one of those? She could learn a lot from Marcus. Time to keep it real.

"Yes. I do like him. A lot. And Dad can't stop me from dating whoever I want." Leah opened the cabinet and sorted through the pills and pain relievers. Which essential oil helped with hangovers? She huffed. Why did they just now have to be out of peppermint? Should she hydrate? Have black coffee? That was what they always did on TV.

"Dad said I have to get my belongings out of here before he gets home."

Mom gasped and slapped a hand to her mouth. "No." She shook her head. "Your father is overreacting. He wouldn't have meant for you to leave."

Leah raised her brows at Melanie for support. Melanie nodded for Leah to continue. Leah had predicted Mom would beg her to stay, so she and Melanie had practiced lines on the drive over.

"It's time to move out. Dad treats me like a toddler, coddling me so I won't get hurt. I need to walk independently without my parents holding me up." Leah softened her tone and tilted her head. "Mom, I appreciate what you've done to help set up my business. Paying no rent has been a real blessing, but I need my independence."

Mom pressed the back of her hand to her mouth and blinked toward the window. "I knew this day would come eventually, but now it's here—" Her voice cracked on the last word. She swiped under her eye and met Leah's gaze. "Sorry. This is not about me. This is about you gaining independence. You're right. It's time." She gave a small smile. "It's not going to be the same without you here—my baby." She flapped a hand in a poor attempt to dry the tears forming. "Not a baby. A big girl. No. I mean, a young lady full of confidence. Smart. Beautiful." Mom rushed around the island and pulled Leah from her stool and into a hug.

Mom sobbed on her shoulder. Leah slowly moved her in a circle, patting her mom's back. She peeked at Melanie and mouthed the words, *Told you.* Mom cried for what seemed an eternity, enough to create a fourth lake in Trinity. What would they call the town now? Quadruple Lakes?

"I need to pack." Leah inched out of Mom's embrace. "Dad will be home in a couple of hours."

Mom dabbed at her cheeks and sniffed. "Take what you can manage today and come back tomorrow when he's at work and pick up the rest. Are you not talking to him?"

Leah resisted an eye roll. "He's kicked me out of home. I don't think he wants to talk to me right now."

"Hmph. Silly man." Mom slapped a hand to her mouth. "Sorry. That was disrespectful."

Melanie grinned. "We can't go disrespecting the sheriff, can we? He might arrest us."

Mom laughed. "He might."

CHAPTER NINE

J ustin added another stack of plastic chairs to the trolley and worked his way through the rows of the mess hall, positioning the chairs so the summer campers could easily move in and out. Three teenage boys from the youth group came with him to help set up the camp early. He nodded to Tim as he passed him. "I'll finish off the right side. You guys can do the left."

"Sure thing." Tim grinned, oozing enthusiasm ... something Justin lacked today.

They had eighty chairs to go. He paused for a beat and rubbed the knot in his neck. Perhaps he needed to slow his pace. He still fumed over what had happened yesterday. Leah hadn't called or apologized. She must be feeling guilty. As she should be.

Was Marcus, the Incredible Hulk, around today? Justin had avoided going near the kitchen. After all, he had no reason to go in there. His job was to set up the mess hall and check the campgrounds. By doing his part, he could show the church board how he was a viable candidate for the youth leader position. The church budget had approved funding for a new staff member, and applications would open soon. Kyla seemed determined to get the position, but something inside him said she wasn't the right person for the job. Not that a youth leader needed a rocky past, but they did need to have compassion for those who struggled. Kyla's reaction to Marcus the other week seemed to say a lot about her judgmental ways. But maybe she saw something he hadn't. Had he lost insight into people?

Metal clanged and echoed. Justin headed toward the front of the hall with his stack of chairs. He could only volunteer for two weeks this summer. He had bills to pay and couldn't take more time from his job. But if the church employed him, even part-time, he could do more.

"Hey, man." Marcus strode toward him like a weightlifting champion. How could Justin compete against the guy? He had muscle on muscle, and the girls all seemed to love Australian accents. Australian men sure seemed popular in Trinity Lakes. He'd never known another town with as many Australians. The town even played Aussie rules football and commemorated Australian events like Anzac Day.

"Hey, bro." Justin slapped his hand into Marcus's beefy one. What was he doing? This guy was not his bro. He was stealing his girlfriend.

Hold on. Leah and he were not official. And they probably would never be now.

Justin stepped back. "What's cooking in the kitchen?"

"We're cooking large batches of soup as an extra to keep the hungry teenagers filled up. We're under the pump today."

Under the pump? Justin shook his head. Must mean pressure or something.

Marcus wiped some sweat off his brow. "I guess you heard what went down yesterday. Did Leah call you?"

"No. But Rhonda Ingalls came to my workshop and told me all about your *date*." He bit out the last word.

"Did she tell you the sheriff wanted to breathalyze his own daughter?" Marcus chuckled.

"You think that's funny?" Justin shifted on his feet and his jaw ticked.

"It wasn't funny at the time. But it sounds ridiculous. Him wanting to breathalyze her. She wasn't even driving. It's not like she's a teenager or anything."

This guy had no clue of how alcohol could destroy a family. It had destroyed Justin's. Destroyed his dad, and now they didn't even know where he lived. "I shouldn't have set you two up together. Stupid thing to do."

"Well, it worked out okay, because Leah has to move out. She won't be under sheriff's watchful eye anymore."

"Huh?"

"Yeah, Daddy Sheriff isn't speaking to her. She's moving in with Melanie and Adam. Love that guy already."

"Found a new friend, hey?" Justin scuffed his sneaker to the linoleum. He and Marcus weren't good friends anyway. They'd only just met. And he regretted every minute of their short friendship. "You'd better get back to your cooking. I have loads to do here."

Marcus frowned and shrugged. "Feel free to pop into the kitchen and grab something to eat."

"Thanks, but I'm good."

"No worries, mate."

Quit with the mate. They were not mates. Not anymore.

Marcus folded his arms across his chest. "Is everything okay? You seem peeved about something. I'm getting chill vibes from you. The freezing kind."

Justin sighed. "I'll be honest with you. I'm not happy about what happened. I'm surprised that Leah is drinking. I didn't think she was that kind of girl." He understood that most people had no problem with alcohol, but he'd made a promise to himself to never touch the stuff because of how it had trapped his father. The wife he chose would need to respect that.

"Have you changed your mind about her?"

"We were only friends. I mean, I did like her, but nothing had started. She wouldn't stand up to her dad and say she wanted to be with me. She decided to walk on eggshells and suck up to him. Is that the kind of woman I want to be with?"

Marcus rubbed at his scruffy chin. "Sounds like you've set high standards for what you want in a partner."

"I certainly have. I want to be in ministry, so I can't just date any girl."

Marcus jerked his head back. "Leah doesn't seem like 'just any girl' to me."

The tendons in Justin's neck tightened.

Marcus slipped his hands into his apron pockets and rocked on his feet, studying him with a frown. "So you wouldn't care if I dated her for real?"

Justin reined in the temptation to punch Marcus. It would be like hitting a brick wall, and he'd be the one left hurting. He had no right to stop Marcus from dating Leah. He didn't have a ring on her finger or anything.

Justin stood back and held up a hand. "She can decide for herself who she wants to date."

"I don't want to step on anyone's toes."

"Aren't you going back to Australia soon? What's the point of starting something when you leave in a few weeks?"

"I live day to day. I don't know what the future holds. But she's nice. She's different from most girls."

Justin had thought so as well until she compromised herself with Marcus. Assuming that was what had actually happened. Had Rhonda really seen them making out?

Marcus slapped Justin on the shoulder in a friendly way, but it was so firm that Justin stumbled to the side to gain his balance. "Well, I'll let you get back to these chairs. I'm gonna continue to the kitchen. See you around." Marcus turned and strode away.

Justin rubbed at his temple. How had he messed things up with Leah? He'd been so wrong about her.

THE BELLBIRD CAFÉ had background music playing. It was meant to be a tinkling of an Australian bellbird but sounded like an old man trying to speak through a mouthful of marbles.

Tim, one of the teens who attended the youth group, sat across from him, practically inhaling his fries. "What's up with you, Justin?" He swiped the back of his hand across his mouth. "You've had this sad look on your face lately." Tim's freckled nose scrunched and released, but his concerned frown remained.

"Dude, adulting is hard. Enjoy the freedom while you're young and don't need to worry about anything."

Tim crossed his arms. "Hey, teenagers worry all the time. And we don't have the freedom adults have. I don't have a car. I can't go wherever I want when I want."

"You have a point there." Justin chuckled.

"Is it girl problems? It's Leah, isn't it?" Tim gave a coy grin. "I know you like her."

Justin shook his head. Tim sounded like his friends, who always teased him about Leah. "There's one big problem standing in the way of Leah and I getting together." He sighed. "The sheriff."

"The sheriff doesn't like you?"

Justin chewed on the inside of his cheek. "That's the feeling I get."

Tim squinted like a miniature detective. "Is it a feeling, or is it something he said?"

Justin glanced around the nearly empty café. None of Sheriff

Thompson's friends were dining in. Did the man even have any friends?

"I'll give you an example. The other day, I helped an old lady who had locked her keys in the car. The sheriff assumed I was breaking in. He took me to the station and was pretty rough about it. He didn't even give me a chance to explain. Must have a prejudice against me." Justin rubbed his temple. "But don't say anything to anyone. I probably shouldn't be talking about it."

"No, it's fine. I'm not going to blab."

Justin hung his head and raked his fingers through his hair. He let out a heavy breath. "The sheriff isn't my only obstacle."

"Who else?"

Justin studied Tim's concerned expression. The boy idolized him.

"Just some guy. He's not going to be around long, but I think Leah likes him."

"What?" Tim sat ramrod straight. "She's dumped you for some other dude?"

Justin waved a hand down. "Lower your voice, bro. We weren't officially an item. We tried to work something out, but it seems we're not meant to be."

Tim punched his fist into his palm. "Who is this guy?"

Justin chuckled. "If you saw him, you'll see you're no match for him. I'm no match for him. He could headbutt me and knock me cold. Not that he'd do that. He's a nice person. That's the unfortunate thing. I don't blame her for liking him. He's talented, funny, lots of muscles, and I set them up together."

"Huh?" Tim gave him a crazy-eyed look. "You set them up?"

Now he'd said too much. "I shouldn't be talking to you about this. I can see a counselor or something if I need to process it all."

"I can listen." Tim threaded his fingers together and rested them on the table. "I can be mature."

Justin heaved a sigh. He did want to get this off his chest and

LL ALWAYS CHOOSE YOU

Tim offered a willing listening ear. And Tim wouldn't judge him for his stupidity. "Are you sure you can keep a secret?"

"Yes, I promise." Tim crossed his heart.

"I don't know why I'm telling you this, but maybe it'll make me feel better."

"It will. It will. Justin, I promise I won't tell anyone."

Justin gulped hard. "It was my stupid idea. I set Leah up on a fake date with an Australian guy, and she fell for him."

Tim's eyes went wider, if that was at all possible. "Dude, that's insane."

"Thanks for the reassurance." Justin dipped a fry into the ketchup.

He shook his head. "No, I mean. Sorry that happened."

"I'm sorry too. Somehow, I do feel a bit better talking to someone about it. It's embarrassing to tell people like Josh or Brandon. They would tease me to no end."

"Your secret is safe with me. And if I see that guy ..." He punched his fist again.

"Good thing I didn't mention names." Justin massaged his forehead. "Anyway, I don't think he's gonna do the right thing by Leah."

"Serves her right. Leah should be punished."

"Hey, dude. Back down. I said we weren't a thing." And they'd never be an item. She'd kissed Marcus and now she was dating him.

———

LEAH SCOOTED into the back row of the church. Marcus settled in next to her, his beefy thighs invading her space. The guy was huge.

Mom and Dad sat near the front of the church, and Pastor Dean made announcements. Marcus fidgeted in his seat.

"Relax." Leah tapped his bouncing knee.

He shook his head. "I haven't been in a church for a while. I'm gonna hear more of this religious stuff at camp."

"You might get stuck in the kitchen."

"I'm not one of the youth. But Chris makes me take breaks to listen to the devotions. He wants me to come back to God or something. Can't remember what he called it."

The lady in front of them turned over her shoulder and glared, placing a forefinger to her lips.

Marcus gritted his teeth in a hilarious Wallace and Gromit smile and whispered, "Sorry."

When the woman faced forward, Leah leaned into Marcus. "It's fine. Don't worry about her." She straightened and tried to focus on the pastor's words. But her mind raced to how she'd manage to exit the building at the end without Dad spotting her.

Why was she stressing about it? It's not like she was dating Marcus or anything. And even if she was, she didn't have to answer to Dad anymore. Her stomach twisted. Despite her age, she still sought her father's approval on decisions. Even when she didn't, she always had the nagging feeling that she should have."

Leah took in a long breath and exhaled her annoyance. The way Dad had treated Marcus made it hard to respect her father. His behavior had been plain rude. She'd made a friend in Marcus. He agreed to come to church, and that was something. Her parents should set a good example and show how Christians were full of grace. They should show Marcus he was accepted.

Leah spotted the back of Justin's head. He sat next to Tim and occasionally glanced about the room. Their gazes met, but he turned without acknowledging her. What was that about?

The music resumed, first the guitar, followed by the piano. Leah stood with the congregation, but Marcus remained seated.

He wasn't going to perform for anyone. Leah sat back down and whispered, "How are you doing?"

"I'm listening to the words." He grinned.

Marcus kept it real, not pretending to be something he wasn't.

Leah smiled and pushed herself to stand. An uneasiness settled in her belly when her gaze wandered back to her father. She loved him and cared what he thought. His disappointment in her hurt. Why did she try so much to please him? It was perfect timing to cut the umbilical cord. She needed to stand on her own.

After the service finished, people milled about chatting, and several headed over to Marcus and welcomed him. Before too long, Leah tugged him away toward the parking lot before Mom and Dad noticed them.

"Do you want to go to the Bellbird Café or try something more upmarket?" Leah pointed the fob and unlocked her Ford Ranger.

Marcus drummed his fingers on the metal roof. "Something else." He gave a crooked grin and slipped into the passenger seat.

Leah mirrored his movements, adjusted her seatbelt, and switched on the ignition. "Have you been to the country club restaurant? It's fancy and quite expensive. But totally delicious."

"I'm all for fine dining. That's what we cook at Bayside View restaurant in Fremantle."

"It's by the beach?"

"Yep. We specialize in fresh local seafood. I'll be a fussy food critic at the country club. I expect the best."

"We'll see." She scanned his clothes. "You look dressed for fine dining." He wore a button-down shirt and dark jeans—possibly the neatest attire she'd seen him in. His face appeared freshly shaven. Interesting—he'd shaved for church.

Marcus clicked on his seatbelt and rubbed his hands. "Let's do this."

Ten minutes later, they climbed the carpeted stairs on the left side of the country club's entrance hall, which led to the restaurant. On the far side, a spacious balcony gave diners a sweeping view of the town and the golf course. At night, Gilbertson Pond would be illuminated by spotlights from the parking lot and streetlamps of the road leading to the club. But during the day, the lake sparkled in all its glory. The mountains lingered in the distance.

Leah approached the hostess, who stood at a small podium, appearing busy but doing little more than blinking with fake eyelashes.

"Do you have a table for two? We don't have a reservation."

The woman ran an overlong black acrylic nail down the reservations list in a gesture reminiscent of every evil witch in every children's cartoon ever made. "We have a table available." She tilted her chin, collected two menus, and led the way to a spot near the windows.

Marcus mimicked the lady, thrusting his head in the air, and rolled his eyes at Leah.

They soon nestled into their seats and chatted casually as they perused the menu.

After the meals were served, Marcus gave a commentary on every aspect of his food—the flavors, the textures, the contrast of sweet and sour. It was like listening to poetry. The guy was so passionate.

Leah leaned back. "You sure know your stuff. I can see food consumes your life."

"It does. Chris has expanded his influence by launching a second restaurant. His business partner and my mate, Kyle, manage the place. So I'm second in charge to Chris. Officially, I'm called a junior chef. But I am the head chef when Chris isn't on shift." He took a sip of sparkling water. "Did you know Chris has a little girl?"

"No."

"He's cut back to three nights now he has a family. He does four lunch shifts instead. Before, he used to work six to seven days a week. Now I'm doing that. No kids. No wife." His expression said he wasn't concerned about the fact. He was younger than Leah, so he likely wasn't looking to settle down anytime soon.

"Do all those hours week after week get tiring?" She loved owning her own business, but still needed downtime.

"Work is hectic, but I love every minute." He scooped a bite of his salmon. "Tell me about you. What are your goals and dreams?"

"I'm living them. When I was sixteen and a vegetarian for a while, I learned all about synthetic chemicals and organic living. I had terrible acne back then, so I changed my diet and tried a few natural alternatives."

"You're beautiful. I never would have guessed you had bad acne."

"Thank you." Marcus might have had bad table manners at her parents' house, but here he was sweet and respectful. "My skin did improve. Then I kept learning new things and slowly made healthier choices. But living in a small town made it difficult to access the products I wanted."

"What about online shopping?"

"I did a lot of online shopping but not for fresh produce. That's what led me to start my business as a supplier. I did a survey first to see if enough people in Trinity would become regular customers and what they wanted me to stock. I was surprised to learn how many people had allergies or health issues. I sell a lot of supplements, too. But mostly, I encourage customers to buy whole foods to get their nutrition."

Marcus nodded. "The food photographer who used to do

our website menu hounds me about me drinking cola. Big sin in her books."

Leah laughed. "Yeah. Sin of all sins in a health fanatic's eyes. What do you mean, used to do your website menu?"

"Melissa moved to America. We haven't found a decent replacement. Chris's wife has taken over the website." He leaned across the table and mock-whispered, "Some of the photos are out of focus." He sat straight and raised his hands. "But who am I to judge? I'm not a photographer."

"But it irks you to see your fabulous creations not showing their full potential."

He pointed his finger. "Exactly. You get it."

Leah pushed her remaining chicken to the side, unable to fit any more in. "What did you think of the church service?"

Marcus crossed his beefy arms and rested them on the table. "I've never met a woman like you."

Her eyes went wide for a beat. How did her question relate to her? Her mind became muddled. Being called a woman by Marcus kind of thrilled her. And he was right. She was a woman.

Marcus must've noticed her surprise. "In a good way. There's something about you that's different. You have a positive outlook on life and don't seem to let things get you down. I mean, what happened the other day is a big thing—your dad's reaction and being kicked out of home." He raised one palm. "But you take it as a nudge to leave the nest and start flapping those wings."

A smile grew on her cheeks. "I like that analogy. I'm a chick who's embarked on her first flight to her new destination."

"See. Like that." Marcus dipped his head and met her eyes. "And you don't seem that cut up about Justin changing his mind."

Leah stilled. Justin had changed his mind? About what? She

mustn't react. She needed to know what Marcus meant and tell her what he knew. "You spoke to him?"

"He's being unfair. How does you having a few drinks stop him from becoming a youth leader? I seriously don't get this church stuff."

Leah's pulse jumped in her throat. She took a sip of water and acted casually as if the news hadn't alarmed her.

Marcus's brow creased and he shook his head. "Man, he looked disappointed in you. Then he went on about how you and he were just friends. I don't get it. Why did he set up this fake dating thing if you weren't something more?"

Leah managed to take a breath and string a sentence together. "We were officially friends. Sounds like I might not be even that at the moment."

Marcus touched her hand. "Hey. It's his loss. This whole debacle is on him, not you. Shows his true character. He suggested you go on the picnic date for others to see. Aside from the hiccup of you getting tipsy—mind the pun—it's what he wanted. The town gossip saw us. So did your dad. Also what Justin wanted. Then you get kicked out of your family home and Justin turns his back on you." Marcus squeezed her hand and let go. "I can't talk about it anymore. I'm angry at Justin. It's what turns me off church people." His frown disappeared. "But you're different. I like you, Leah. You're the real deal. I don't feel judged by you."

Leah touched her sternum. "Oh, I'm not that amazing. I mean, I try to be understanding and not judge people. Even if I haven't lived what they've been through." Compassion filled her heart. "You had a rough start to life, didn't you?"

Marcus looked to the golf course outside then met her gaze. "Yeah. Didn't have the best time growing up. But the past is behind me. I'm carving out my future."

"Good for you." Leah twisted her cloth napkin. "About Justin. He wants to be the next youth leader. So it looks bad if he keeps company with a drunkard." She rolled her eyes. "If only Rhonda hadn't been at the lake that day."

"I didn't think that little cider would get anyone drunk. I feel awful. If I'd known how much it would affect you, I would've said more. I figured you knew." He paused and gave her a questioning look. "Do you even have cider with alcohol here in the States?"

"I think it's called hard cider." Leah waved a hand. "The fake dating thing was a big mistake. Justin should have tried to get to know my dad so Dad could have confidence in Justin. Then ask for a blessing."

"Do I need to ask your dad for his blessing if I want to date you?"

Leah blinked and stumbled her words. "Oh, it's more of a respect thing, not an absolute. It's tradition to ask the father's permission before proposing." She bit her bottom lip. "But I won't ask Dad's permission to date someone. Not anymore, anyway."

"Sounds about right."

She sighed. "I'm annoyed at him, but I do love and respect my father."

Marcus shook his head. "I don't respect the way he treated you. That wasn't fair."

"Jesus isn't like that, Marcus. Do you know any of the Bible stories?"

"You're going to preach to me now?" Marcus laughed.

She smiled. "No. I want you to know that Jesus got bad-mouthed because he hung out with the tax collectors and sinners. My dad is not a good representation of Christians. At least, not when it comes to you. Or Justin."

"I get it. Between you and Chris and his wife Cassie, I do see the difference." His Adam's apple bobbed in his neck. "I didn't have a good relationship with my parents. Dad was a harsh man. We don't see each other much. Maybe once a year at Christmas, or at weddings and funerals."

"That's sad."

"Probably why I went off track as a teenager. I didn't have a good role model—until Chris stepped in. He helped me set goals, kept me busy working, and taught me how to earn an honest living."

"Sounds like a great guy to have in your life."

"Without him and Cassie, I don't know where I'd be. Probably prison."

Leah's jaw dropped, and then she shut it quickly.

"I was in a dark place at sixteen. But by the time I turned eighteen, I became an award-winning chef. I've had amazing reviews in popular food magazines across Australia."

"And you've worked hard for it."

"Sometimes it's difficult to relax. This holiday is a challenge for me. I'm looking forward to getting into the kitchen but having this Sunday off is nice."

"Good. Summer camp is supposed to be a good balance of work and fun."

"Should be good to experience an American summer camp. I've heard so much about them. We don't have long camps where I'm from. Ours last maybe a week over Easter or after Christmas."

"Right."

"I would take time off if I had an American friend come tour Australia. We have immaculate beaches. I live right near the sea. We enjoy fresh lobster, crayfish, and barramundi. I love going to the fish market and selecting the best produce for the restaurant."

"Sounds amazing."

"It is. The locals go to Fremantle markets for organics. The people there are either hippies or rich people who can afford organic food. It's expensive in Australia."

"Organic isn't cheap here, either. But if we don't look after our health and pay more now, we'll pay later in medical bills."

He nodded. "And you can taste more flavor in the organic fruit. You know that feeling of disappointment when you bite into a peach or plum, and it's bland and floury? Goes straight into the trash. But not when it's organic. Always full of flavor."

"They'll probably find a way to genetically modify fruit to have artificial flavors or something in the future."

"You better believe it." Marcus folded his arms on the table. "How is your business doing?"

"The first year, I took on a big loan for all the equipment and setting up shop, but I've paid that off now. In the second year, I broke even. Now I'm making a profit, so I can pay myself a small wage even after I've covered rent and bills. Occasionally, I have Nina filling in for me to give me a break."

"Good on you for sticking it out. Not everyone will give a business a go and take a risk."

She studied Marcus. Getting involved with a guy who lived on the other side of the planet would be a huge risk. Leah shook her head and kept those silly ideas at bay.

CHAPTER TEN

After the church service, Justin wove through the crowded church hall, searching for Leah, but tried not to be too obvious. He nodded hellos to several people he knew and avoided getting caught up in conversation. He had to determine whether she was with Marcus or not and see if she was flirting with the oversized chef.

People hugged or shook hands. Some stood in groups laughing in animated conversation. He spotted a few teenagers piling their plates high from the buffet table. The scent of cinnamon rolls, apple pie, and casseroles wafted past his nose, but he wouldn't get distracted by the growl in his belly. Where was Leah?

The fluorescent lights aggravated the headache at his temples. He only got headaches when he was stressed. Justin passed the posters and flyers about the upcoming bazaar and charity drive on the notice board, then bumped into something hard.

Flip. He'd chest-bumped Sheriff Thompson, and not in a bro-like manner.

"Sorry, sir. I wasn't looking where I was going."

He frowned. "I sensed that." He fisted his chest. "Right here."

Was the guy making a joke? By the stern line of his lips, probably not. He was a complicated person to work out.

A smirk broke free from the sheriff, but it disappeared just as quickly. "I came over to talk to you."

Justin shifted on his feet. "How can I help, Sheriff?"

Deep lines creased his forehead. "Call me Martin. I'm not on duty."

Justin collected his jaw from the floor. Were he and the sheriff now on a first-name basis?

Rhonda floated past them, red-painted lips smiling in a suspiciously over-friendly way.

Martin Thompson lowered his voice. "I need to talk to you somewhere private."

"Sure. Where do you want to go?"

"Let's go to the gardens." The sheriff turned, and Justin followed close behind.

Tim gave him a weird look and mouthed the words, "Everything okay?"

Justin shrugged and scurried to keep up with the sheriff's stride. They reached the edge of the grassed area and stood under a large oak. No one should be able to overhear them.

The sheriff faced Justin. "I've made a terrible mistake."

Justin remained silent. Had the sheriff been convicted about how he'd mistreated Justin at the lake the other day? He sure had shoved him hard into Mrs. Darcy's car.

"I told Leah not to rush into a relationship with you, and now look at what's happened." He raised a palm, gesturing to the building.

Justin darted a glance around the garden and back to the sheriff's worried face. "What happened?"

"Crocodile Dundee." The sheriff shook his head like that was a perfect explanation.

Justin raked his fingers through his hair. "And why are you telling me this?"

The sheriff let out a dramatic sigh. "I'm apologizing." He scuffed the grass with his polished shoe. The guy probably didn't apologize to anyone.

"I'm sorry for judging you harshly for what happened when you were a teen."

"I'd figured you still held that against me."

"I'm the one who saw you speeding, and you didn't pull over when my lights were flashing," he said sternly.

"I was sixteen. Ten years have passed."

"Correct." His brow twitched. "But I had another prejudice against you. An unfair one."

Unease rippled through Justin's chest. He didn't want to hear why, but they needed to move past whatever Sheriff Thompson —no, Martin—had against him.

"Your father and I went to school together. He was well known as the school bully. That's one of the reasons I wanted to grow up and be a policeman, a man of the law. To lock up punks like your dad."

Justin stumbled a step back. He despised the bad name his dad had left him. It took years to get people to overlook his rotten DNA. "I'm nothing like my father." His tone held great conviction.

"I can see that now." Sheriff massaged his forehead. "As I said, I'm sorry. And I see you in a different light in comparison to Marcus, who isn't walking with the Lord. My daughter got drunk with him—something she wouldn't usually do." Sheriff frowned and dipped his head. "As far as I can see, Marcus doesn't have any morals. And I don't want to lose Leah to another country. This is a disaster."

"I can imagine it would be heartbreaking." It was for Justin. "Can I ask why you're telling me all this?"

Sheriff met his gaze. "I need your help. You need to win Leah back. Show her you're the better choice."

"I hoped she knew that already." He shrugged. "Now I'm not so sure. Anyway, she's an adult. She'll decide for herself." Assuming the sheriff's apology was genuine, and he would let Leah decide.

"Leah needs to know you're willing to fight for her."

"Fight Marcus? He could squash me like a bug just by sitting on me. I can't fight him."

"I don't mean that kind of fight. Show her how much she matters. You might not believe this, but I did silly romantic things to win Leah's mother over. I even wrote poetry. Worse, I sang to her and couldn't hold a note."

Justin held back a chuckle.

"I learned to play the guitar. Well, three basic chords. I serenaded her."

"How did that go?"

"She burst out laughing."

Justin let go of a smile. He could imagine it in his head.

"But it worked. She thought it was sweet." He gripped the back of his neck. "That's the thing I'm kicking myself about. I found a poem from you in Leah's room. I panicked at the time, but now she's falling for an Australian. I could lose her to another country. I admit I'm overbearing at times, but I don't want her to get hurt. She's precious to me—my only daughter. It's different when you have an only child. They're your whole world, and if their life crumbles, you crumble."

Justin had never seen this side of the sheriff before. It was a privilege, really. Justin cleared his throat. "Martin." His name felt weird to speak. "I was disappointed about it as well. I was surprised. But I can't stop her from making decisions."

"You can't just let her go like that. Marcus is not a good influence."

He shook his head. "Sir, I'm sorry."

"I thought I could come to you for help. I apologized for

judging and holding the past against you. Kids do stupid things. I know. I've put Leah on a pedestal and thought no one could match her. That was wrong."

Wow. Justin couldn't believe his ears. Did he have a severe case of ear wax? "What about how you treated me like a criminal the other day?" The words were out before he could contemplate his question. But the sheriff needed to see that he'd mistreated Justin when he accused him of breaking into Mrs. Darcy's car.

Sheriff rubbed the scruff on his chin. It was unusual for the man not to shave, even on weekends. Justin had never seen him unkempt. He must've had a rough sleep worrying about Leah. *Join the no-sleep club, buddy.*

"I'm sorry about that too." He dropped his arms to his side, looking defeated. "See, I can humble myself and apologize. I was rough on you and didn't let you have a chance to explain yourself. Again, I judged you because of your father. This morning in church, I let all that go. It's embarrassing to say how long I've taken to forgive that man. But you've changed my outlook and given me hope in young people. You've redeemed the Perry name."

His lungs expanded to their maximum capacity, and he let out a slow, steady breath. With those last five words, Justin grew a few inches taller. He extended his hand. "I accept your apology."

Sheriff engulfed his palm and pulled Justin into a manly hug. The usually stiff and formal policeman gave Justin firm pats on the back and then pushed him back upright. What had just happened? The sheriff had hugged him. Woah.

"Thanks, Martin. I'm glad we cleared that up."

"Me too. Please think about my request." Sheriff gave a curt nod and strode away.

Okay, so maybe too many touchy-feely, happy vibes going on. The sheriff needed to regain his cold façade.

Justin turned and observed the remaining crowd lingering in the parking lot. He didn't feel like chatting with his friends. They liked to joke around too much, and Justin wasn't in the mood. Not today. Sure, joking with his friends might get him out of this funk, but he needed time to process what the sheriff had suggested.

Should he go after Leah?

Or should he wait for her to wake up and choose him?

————

LEAH PLONKED herself on the leather couch in the B&B's living room. Though it was still summer, the unlit fireplace created a cozy atmosphere. The cream-painted walls and rich burgundy curtains warmed the room, inviting Leah to curl up and rest. But this wasn't the time for that. Book club night required concentration. Leah let out a weary sigh.

"Long day?" Hannah smiled and waved from the other side of the room.

"You could say that." Leah scanned the living area. Only six women had showed up to the book club. Tabby had messaged that it would be a smaller group, so they weren't venturing to the Bellbird Café this month.

Tabby entered from the kitchen carrying a platter of cheeses, cold meats, crackers, and vegetables sticks. "Have some snacks to revive your weary soul." Tabby playfully presented the dish to Leah then withdrew it as Leah reached out a hand. A smirk crept up her cheeks. "Wait a minute. Some of these aren't organic."

Leah rolled her eyes. "The joke is getting old, you guys. Hand them over. I need some energy if I'm going to string a sentence together."

Tabby placed the platter on the coffee table beside a selection of goodies. Yes, Leah had provided certified organic fruit.

But she had extra produce, and she couldn't let it go to waste. Not at the prices she paid.

Hannah snatched a cracker and dipped it into the cream cheese dip before popping it into her mouth. She crossed her legs at the ankles and tilted her head at Leah. "Is there anything else bothering you, other than being tired?"

Leah's gaze darted between Tabby and Hannah. "Justin hasn't called me. It's been ten days."

"Have you tried to call him?" Tabby poured her lemon soda into a glass.

"On the night of the picnic incident. He didn't pick up or return my call. Marcus says he's disappointed in me for getting tipsy. That's the only reason I can think of for why he's avoiding me."

Hannah pulled out this month's book club choice from her tote bag and rested it on her lap, holding the edges. "But has he left for summer camp already?"

"Probably. He's only attending a couple of weeks this year."

"Then why don't you visit the camp and see if he ignores you there?"

"I need to look after my shop. My worker is at camp this year."

"What about Melanie?" Tabby lifted a palm. "She could do her marketing online and work from your store for the day."

"Maybe. I feel like I've already asked a lot of her lately. I overheard her and Adam having a little argument the other night. When I thought it was safe to come out to get something from the kitchen, they were making out in the living room." She winced. "Awkward. I stayed in my room for the rest of the night."

Hannah laughed. "That would be uncomfortable, living with a newlywed couple. They need their space to argue, then kiss and make up."

"I agree." Tabby leaned back in her seat and turned toward

Leah. "Why don't you stay here? I'll give you a good price."

"If I can't find a rental in the next two weeks, I'll have to take up your offer."

"Pftt. You make it sound like it's some two-star motel on a no-number highway." Tabby grinned.

"Oh, I don't mean to sound ungrateful. Your B&B is gorgeous, but it's well out of my budget. I need to get a cheap rental."

"I'll give you a discount in exchange for your help in the evenings with the occasional late check-in."

"Sounds promising."

"I actually don't have room for you in the guest wing. I'm fully booked until August—thank goodness. But I've almost cleared out Gran's room, thanks to Logan. You could stay there." Tabby reached for another cracker. "Logan and I can finish clearing out the bedroom this week if you don't mind that the bathroom needs work."

Leah shrugged. "I suppose." She palmed her forehead. "I feel like such a baby, not knowing how to be independent. I'm afraid of the unknown and living near strangers." Justin seemed much older and had it together. Except now he looked down on her. She could have done with his help about now. He usually had good advice, and he would've joined her to hunt for somewhere to live. He was always like that with his friends. For a while, she assumed she had taken the position of his best friend. Not anymore.

"Enough about me." Leah puffed the bangs hanging in her eyes. "What's going on between you and the Kiwi football player? If he's helped you clear out your Gran's room, you've obviously been spending a lot of time together."

Tabby coughed on her food. Her face went red, and tears formed in her eyes. She patted her chest and tried to speak, but no words emerged.

Hannah laughed. "Just the mention of him is making your

heart pound in your chest."

Leah joined in the laughter. "I'm sure that's a line from one of our books. Oh, if Kyla only knew we were reading a romance novel this month, she'd be jumping behind the pulpit and waving her finger at us."

Tabby swiped at her mouth. "Maybe that's why I can't get Logan out of my head. It's this romance novel giving me ideas." She stabbed a finger in the direction of the book on Hannah's lap. "I blame Becky Kinzer for writing such descriptive scenes that make you feel like one of the characters."

"You tell yourself that." Hannah laughed. "You can't stop talking about him at work."

"You keep asking. Okay, I will admit I've had a crush on Logan Wylde for half of forever. But I squash those ideas as quick as they come. There's no point. He's going to leave. He's all about traveling the country and the world. I have a job here, and I'm needed at the B&B."

Leah pouted her bottom lip. "Oh. That's sad. I could see you and Logan together." She lifted her palms. "I don't know what it is exactly. It's more than chemistry. You two have something else going on."

"Destiny." Hannah sat straighter. "Is that the word you were looking for? They seem destined for each other."

Leah's lips twitched to one side. "I wouldn't want to put ideas in your head that it was God's plan or anything. That's not my place to say." She tilted her head toward Tabby. "Have you prayed about it? Do you feel a peace about him?"

Tabby fiddled with her sleeve and dipped her chin. "It's hard to hear from God when my emotions are involved. I can't get my head to shut up when I think about if we're right for each other. I can't see how it would work, but I wish it could."

Hannah leaned forward and squeezed Tabby's knee. "I get it. These are the challenges of a single woman. Who is Mr. Right? Is that even a thing?"

Leah shook her head. "We should change the name of our book club to Single Women's Strategy Night. We talk about books five percent of the night and the rest is about our lack of love lives."

Hannah chuckled. "I can brag now I'm not lacking. But I do have dramas. Mom was so horrible to Joel at the last family dinner that he doesn't want to come to another one. I don't know why Mom hates him so much."

"Who could hate Joel? He's so nice." Leah shook her head.

Hannah tapped her book. "I agree. Right, let's focus." Hannah scanned the room, which was missing several regulars, but she did the motion anyway as if we were all present. "Who read this month's book to the end?"

Becky and Leah shot their hands in the air, but Tabby's only flew half-mast.

Leah widened her eyes at Tabby. "Come on. Don't tell fibs. Did you finish it or not? We do believe in forgiveness in this room, so it's okay if you haven't." She smirked.

Tabby lifted one shoulder. "I may have skipped a few pages to get to the good parts. But doubt I missed much."

Hannah waved a hand. "Don't worry about it. This isn't an English class, and we aren't getting graded. I barely finished but managed to speed read the last few chapters this afternoon."

"I'm glad I'm not the only one." Tabby rustled through her purse and pulled out her e-reader.

Leah struggled to focus on the book discussion as her mind drifted to Justin. Maybe she should call him again to know for sure what was going on in that head of his. Perhaps she was too traditional in thinking the man should instigate the relationship. Wasn't that what got them in this trouble in the first place? All because she had to keep to Dad's traditions in getting his approval. What if Dad's judgment was way off? Did she still have to honor him and not date who she thought was right for her?

CHAPTER ELEVEN

Two weeks later, Leah still hadn't heard a word from Justin. Who would break the ice first?

Leah opened the back roller door of Trinity Organics and strolled through the shop, fingering shelves for dust. Nina had done an okay job yesterday. Leah unlocked the front door and placed the chalkboard with today's special of chicken soup on the sidewalk. As she spun around, her jaw slackened, and a gasp escaped her lips.

"Oh my word." She slapped a hand to her mouth.

Graffiti was scrawled in black spray paint on the white paneling, defaming her name. "Who would do this?"

The words accused her of being a two-timer, followed by several curse words. Someone had heard about her and Marcus —someone who knew that she and Justin liked each other.

Leah dragged a palm down her cheek. She needed to get rid of this vandalism quickly before her customers saw it. Panic rose in her chest as she shielded her eyes and glanced across the road. Thankfully, she'd arrived extra early this morning, ready to receive her delivery from Walla Walla.

Leah slipped out her cell phone from her jeans pocket and,

with shaky hands, dialed Tabby's number. She shoved a finger-nail between her teeth and chewed the last bit of nail that she'd been trying to regrow. The last couple of weeks had been nerve-wracking. She would not report this to her dad. He would be furious, and she wasn't speaking to him at the moment, so it wasn't an option anyway. The last thing she wanted was to be taken to the police station to give a statement.

"You're calling early. What's the matter?" Tabby's voice held concern.

"Do you have any leftover white paint in your garden shed? The one we used on the veranda railing would be perfect."

"I have about half a gallon left. Why's that?"

Leah rubbed her forehead and looked at the obscenities. "Oh, you wouldn't believe it. Trinity Organics has been vandal-ized. Graffiti. Someone has said the most awful things about me."

Tabby gasped. "That's terrible, Leah. I hope my paint hasn't expired. But it will do for now."

"Yeah, that's what I'm thinking. I'll take some photos for insurance purposes just in case, and paint over this before any customers see."

"All right, I'll be right down. Don't worry, Leah. We'll get this sorted out."

Leah ended the call. A tiny bit of relief settled over her, knowing her friend would come to the rescue.

Leah spun around at the sound of footfalls, and her stomach dropped. Just when all would be well, the second most annoying person on the planet approached. Rhonda came in as the gold finalist for starting rumors by a hairsbreadth, and the woman jogging Leah's way held the silver medal. Why did Kyla pick today for a morning jog through town?

Kyla's perk posture, with her cutesy ponytail swinging side to side, headed in Leah's direction. How could she cover these awful words before Kyla saw them?

Kyla's eyes lit up when she noticed Leah standing on the sidewalk. Leah grabbed the blackboard sign and shuffled it forward. Hopefully, Kyla would have to jog around and not glance to her left. Leah gritted her teeth in an attempted smile, offered Kyla a quick wave, and dipped her head, pretending to be extremely busy positioning the important sign. Out of her peripheral vision, Kyla slowed to a stop, placed her hands on her hips, and puffed several breaths.

"Leah, how are you this morning?"

"Um, good. Thanks." Leah's voice wobbled slightly. Dread clogged her throat when Kyla glanced at the white paneling, scrolled with graffiti.

"What in the world? Two-timing—? This is disgusting." Kyla's eyes nearly sprang out of their sockets. "Leah! What is this all about? Who would say such a thing about you? Your dad is going to be furious."

Leah scraped her teeth over her bottom lip. She tried to bide her time on how to answer.

Kyla tilted her head to one side. "Is this about the Australian chef? I heard the rumors. I'm disappointed with you, Leah." She pointed to the graffiti. "Now your reputation is on the line."

"Excuse me?" She fisted one hip. "I haven't done anything wrong."

"I thought you were in love with Justin. Why on earth were you on a date with a tourist?"

"It wasn't like that, Kyla. Justin knew about it, and it was his idea." Leah slapped a hand to her mouth. She knew better than to share personal information with Kyla. The woman would use it against her.

Kyla's brows shot up. "Justin knew you were going on a date with someone else, and he approved?"

"Marcus is a mutual friend." Well, he was a mutual friend. Justin hasn't spoken to him much either. "And we did nothing wrong. Rhonda Ingalls twisted the story. And now my dad is super angry and kicked me out." And she shouldn't have said that, either. Not to Kyla.

"You've been kicked out of your home?"

Would Kyla stop acting like a parrot and repeating everything Leah said? "I'm twenty-four years old. It's time I moved out of home. My business loan has nearly been paid off, and I need to become independent."

Kyla gestured toward the graffiti. "Who do you think did this?"

"I don't know—someone who doesn't understand the truth. But anyway, it's none of anyone's business. Tabby's coming to sort this out." Leah placed her palms in a prayer pose. "Please, Kyla. I know we're not the closest of friends. But please don't make this any worse. Don't tell anyone. Tabby will be here soon, and we'll clean this before any of my customers see. This town is too small to let things fly. It could affect my business."

Kyla crossed her arms and lifted her chin. "You're right, Leah. We aren't the closest of friends. And I'm not making you any promises. I let my yes be yes, and my no be no. I'm going to finish my run." She flicked her ponytail like a snobby show jumper. "Goodbye."

Leah's mouth fell open as Kyla jogged away past the shopfronts of Main Street. She was a piece of work, that one. Hopefully, Kyla had the decency to keep her mouth shut. Doubtful.

Tabby arrived within five minutes, with a paint tin in hand and two brushes. Leah engulfed her in a hug and squeezed the life out of her friend. "You're a lifesaver. Thanks for coming so quickly."

Tabby pulled back, and concern filled her eyes. "Of course, anytime. But I can't stay long.—I've left Dad in charge of the guest's breakfast. Let's get this over with." She eyed the panels. "This is disgusting, Leah. I'm so sorry this happened to you."

Tabby bent down and proceeded to remove the lid with a

knife. Both girls got to work and swirled their brushes into the paint. In silence, they worked quickly to cover the defaming words.

Once the last bit of black spray paint was invisible, Tabby faced Leah, arms dropped to her side. "No one will ever know."

Except at least one other person had seen the graffiti. Should she tell Tabby about Kyla?

"Who do you think could have done this, Leah? Why would someone want to damage your reputation? You don't think Justin would have anything to do with it, do you?"

Leah straightened. "Of course not. Justin wouldn't let a swear word pass his lips. He's not like that."

"Who else, then? One of Justin's friends?"

"I don't think he hangs around those types of friends. But maybe someone who knows the situation and looks up to Justin."

Tabby's eyes widened, and she shot her index finger in the air. "Perhaps one of the youth he mentors."

Leah nodded. "You could be right. If I tell Justin, he might guess who did it."

"It would give you an excuse to talk to him."

"He might feel justified when he finds out. He's annoyed and avoiding me."

Tabby shook her head. "You don't know that for sure. Maybe he's waiting for you to reach out. It doesn't always have to be the guy chasing the girl. Perhaps he needs to hear it from your mouth that you still want to be together."

Leah scrunched her nose. "I don't want to be with someone who's so quick to judge. He should be asking me for the facts and not making assumptions. Justin should know me better by now."

CHAPTER TWELVE

J ustin nestled into the office chair opposite the pastor. Old portraits and paintings of past ministers hung on the walls. A bookcase stood against a red wall, filled with small plaques and framed newspaper articles.

Pastor Dean rolled his chair away from his desk, crossed his legs at the ankles, and steepled his fingers on his lap. Why had the pastor called him in for a chat? A possible position as the youth leader?

"Justin, thank you for meeting me this morning. How do you feel your time at this year's summer camp went?"

"Excellent. Everything ran smoothly. The kids seemed to enjoy the discussions and stayed engaged. It was great seeing the surrounding towns join us again." He lifted his chin. "I would've stayed longer, but I need to pay the bills."

The pastor rested his elbows on the arms of his chair. The leather squeaked as he leaned forward. "What did you think of the Australian team?"

Justin straightened, and uneasiness coiled around his spine. "Do you mean the kitchen hands?"

Pastor Dean frowned. "The local kids were the kitchen

hands. I'm talking about the chefs from Australia—Chris and Marcus." Pastor Dean quirked a brow.

Did he know something? "Food was great. I didn't hear any complaints."

The ticking of the wall clock echoed through the room. Its hands pointed to the hour but only by a few minutes.

The pastor massaged his chin. "One concern was raised, but it didn't happen at camp. Something has been brought to my attention, and I think you know about it."

Justin gulped hard. "Something that didn't happen at camp?"

"Look, Justin, what happens in town is not my business, but I know you would like to take more of a leadership role in the youth team. You've made it clear that you want to apply for the youth leader position when we open applications. Choosing to be part of my leadership team means transparency and me speaking into your life." Pastor Dean's voice was low and gravely. He had a way of enunciating his words that brought a vibration to them. "I heard about Leah's incident with the Australian chef at the lake. Most people in Trinity Lakes have likely heard because of a certain person who witnessed the event."

Was the pastor concerned about Justin's association with Leah? "I haven't talked to Leah about it. It's not any of my business who she dates."

"Isn't it? You had nothing to do with her 'dating' Marcus." He used air quotes.

What did the pastor know? Had the Holy Spirit revealed their scheme to Pastor Dean? Had Leah told someone, who then told someone else, who told another until it came to the pastor's attention? "I did introduce Marcus to Leah."

"I had the impression you were in love with the young lady. What doesn't make sense to me is why you encouraged her to see Marcus if what Kyla says is true."

Justin ground his back molars. Now it all made sense. Kyla

wanted to be a youth leader and would do anything to win the role. Kyla had gone to the lowest of lows by reporting this to the pastor. Unless God was using Kyla to bring the secret from the darkness into the light where it could be dealt with.

"I made a big mistake in introducing Marcus to Leah. I trusted him, and I trusted Leah. At first, it was a bit of fun to show the sheriff I'm not as bad as some. But even though I'm on better terms with the sheriff, I've lost Leah in the process."

"We also need to put your chances of becoming a youth leader on hold. Your actions are not setting a good example for our youth. Our leaders need to live a life of integrity and honesty." The pastor let out a long breath. "Justin, you are a young man, and we are all about supporting and discipling you for growth. I don't think you're ready to take the leadership role. I advise you not to apply when the position opens."

Like a bullet wound to the heart, Justin rubbed the ache in his chest. "Are you serious?"

"Very serious," Pastor said bluntly.

Justin dragged a hand down his cheek. "I respect your decision and your wisdom in this. I would like to continue to get more mentoring and discipleship from you. I hope you'll see I can and will make the necessary changes, and I can be trusted." Justin spoke with confidence, but inside, he trembled as emotion rose. How could a silly prank become such a disaster? He sure had learned his lesson the hard way.

———

"THAT'LL BE TWENTY-EIGHT DOLLARS. Is that on card or cash?" Leah pushed the paper grocery bag to the side and smiled at one of her regular customers.

Margie handed over a silver credit card. "Card." She peeked at the glass dome at the end of the counter. "Do you mind if I add a raw mint slice?"

"They're irresistible, aren't they?" Leah took an eco-friendly container from under the counter and retrieved a cashew mint slice. She placed a napkin and bamboo spoon inside the takeout box as well. She added up the new total and charged Margie's card.

Margie tapped her chin. "While I'm here, I should take some chicken broth. I've been reading up on the benefits. Gotta look after these old bones." Margie wriggled her crooked forefinger.

Leah grimaced. "I've run out of soup today. I've stopped making large batches since the weather has warmed up."

She waved a hand. "No problem. I'll buy the stock powder next time I'm in." Margie glanced over her shoulder. "I don't want to keep you from serving other customers."

A tall young lady with red hair smiled at Margie. "Take your time. I can wait."

"I'm in here every second day." She nodded, turned back to her grocery bag, and gathered it into her chest. "Thank you, Leah. See you soon, sweetheart."

Leah smiled as her next customer stepped forward with two items.

"Nice shop you have here." The girl with the posh accent glanced about the store. "Has it been here long?"

"Two years." Leah scanned the first item, but her brain couldn't work out if the accent was Australian or American. "And what brings you to Trinity Lakes?"

She smiled awkwardly. "Long story. But I spent some years here as a kid."

Leah frowned. "You look close to my age. How come we didn't cross paths when you lived here before?"

"My parents are missionaries, so I was home educated."

"Oh, I bet that was fun—work until lunchtime and have the rest of the day off."

"No way." Her eyes went wide. "I wanted to finish as soon as possible so my parents could go back to the mission field. I graduated two years early."

"I didn't think homeschoolers graduated."

"It's up to the parents, but some groups make a big fuss about it, and others don't. Mine didn't, but I had a small gathering and cake."

"Nice. I'm Leah, by the way. You're not related to Nicole Kidman, are you?" Leah laughed to break the ice. The girl seemed a little intense, the serious type.

"Hallie. And no, Nicole doesn't have hair as red as mine, or as many freckles."

Leah waved a hand. "She probably wears a ton of makeup. All the actresses do." Leah placed a liquid iron supplement bottle into the grocery bag. "I bet the American guys dig your accent and your all-natural Aussie look."

Hallie's brows shot up. "No guys are into me. And I'm not actually Australian. But I've heard you're into Australian men." Hallie slapped a hand to her mouth. "Sorry. That sounded awful. I shouldn't listen to gossip." Her face went red like a bright air balloon.

Leah shook her head and scrunched the paper bag shut instead of folding it neatly at the top like usual. "It's fine. The rumors will die down eventually. It comes with the package of living in Trinity Lakes."

"So it's just a rumor?"

Leah nudged the bag to the edge of the counter and breathed out a heavy breath. "My fling with the Australian chef?" She rolled her eyes. "Yes, it's a lie. You're one of the first people to ask me for the truth. Everyone else is making assumptions and giving me weird looks at church." She leaned forward and lowered her voice. "Can you keep a secret?"

Hallie held up a hand. "If it's something sinister or immoral, don't tell me. I don't want to know your secret."

Wow. Leah swallowed. Something inside her wanted to push

through and ask not-Nicole Kidman for her random thoughts anyway. "Do you think it's immoral if I fake-dated someone?"

Hallie shifted on her feet. "Depends on what your motive is, I suppose."

What was her motive? To get her father to see that Justin was a decent guy. Well, that failed.

"But I'd rather not know." Hallie interrupted her thoughts. "Then I don't need to lie to anyone to keep your secret."

"Sure. I respect that." Leah punched the cost of Hallie's order into the till. Her eyes drifted to the window at the far end of the shop. Outside, the sun had unlocked its grip on the day, peeking through the bare branches of the trees and casting its golden hue over the street. "Nineteen dollars and twenty-five cents, please. Cash or card?"

"Card." Hallie opened her mobile case and held out a gray card. "I hope I have enough in that one. If not, I have another." Hallie watched as the machine beeped a confirmation of her payment.

Leah ripped off a printed receipt and handed it to Hallie. "Do you go to a particular church in town?"

"Trinity Life Church. My family have been friends with the Ladan family for years."

"Oh, so you know Josh?"

A hue of pink flushed Hallie's cheeks. "Yes. Very well."

Leah dipped her head and raised a brow. She nearly said something, but Hallie seemed the reserved type. Josh was too much of a clown. No, that would never work.

"Say hi to Josh for me then."

Hallie's smile returned. "Will do."

CHAPTER THIRTEEN

L eah leaned over the railing overlooking the Trinity Lakes Golf Club. The scent of fresh grass clippings and a hint of pine permeated the night air.

Tabby swirled her glass of lemon soda before tipping her head back and taking several gulps. She joined Leah at the railing and bumped her hip into Leah's.

"Are you having a good night?" Tabby asked.

Leah gave it a dramatic sigh. "I am. Bethany's party has been fun so far. But it's awkward knowing Justin is here."

"Have you run into him yet?" Tabby turned to face Leah.

"No, he's avoiding me."

"Are you sure?"

"I went to the buffet table while he was there, and he disappeared in a blink of an eye. I assume he's doing everything to avoid me tonight."

"Why don't you approach him and say hi? See what happens."

Tabby looked over the railing entwined with fairy lights. A few young adults mingled at the other end of the balcony.

"I'm not going to chase a man. If Justin wants to talk to me, he knows where I am. I have a shop in town. He's had plenty of opportunities to come and visit me."

"That's true." Tabby spun and leaned her back into the rail, facing the double glass doors. "Shall we go back inside? It's starting to get a little bit cool."

Leah shrugged her thin cardigan over her shoulders and hugged the collar to her neck. "You're right. It is cold out here."

Leah followed Tabby into the ballroom rented for Bethany's birthday party.

As Leah stepped inside, a blast of hip-hop music greeted her. A DJ bobbed his head in time with the beat, and lights flashed all around him. Friends danced on a raised dance floor with a disco ball shining over them causing a dreamy effect.

At the edge, Hannah seemed in deep conversation with her sister, Becky. Leah doubted she'd be able to get Hannah to dance. She loved most sports, but dancing was not her thing.

"I'll be right back." Leah turned to Tabby. "I need to go to the bathroom."

"I'll see you at the smorgasbord table. I'm going to grab more dessert."

Leah made her way to the restrooms, dodging people left and right. She needed to snap out of her surly mood and shake off the uneasy feeling of being out of favor with Justin.

As if the mere thought of him sent the man a notification to find her, Justin exited the male restrooms. He paused in his tracks and forced a grin. "Hey, Leah. How are you doing?"

Leah's throat clogged. How should she answer the question? It was a simple greeting, but she couldn't blurt how frustrated she was. Why hadn't he called or visited her shop?

Leah tucked a strand of hair behind her ear and swung her arms behind her back. "I'm okay. What have you been up to?"

Justin raked a hand through his hair and glanced left and right. No one was coming or going. Was he ashamed to be associated with her? Most of her friends hadn't said anything about the picnic incident. But with Kyla spreading rumors, they'd all know. And some would be judging her.

"Nothing much. After my rostered time at summer camp, I buried myself in work. We got behind when I had time off."

Leah scraped her teeth over her bottom lip and nodded.

Justin dug one hand into his jeans pocket and rocked on his heels. "What about you? Busy?"

This conversation was as awkward as balancing on a tightrope. They'd usually banter and joke. It was never uneasy. "Same here. Nothing much."

Justin dipped his chin toward the carpet before locking eyes with Leah. "How's Marcus?" Bitterness filled his tone. He wasn't interested in Marcus.

"Why don't you ask him yourself? He's here working in the restaurant."

Justin's face paled for a beat. His eyebrows angled inward. "What is he doing working at the country club?"

"He's a workaholic who is supposed to be on vacation but can't help being in the kitchen. He toured for a few days after camp, but the head chef here offered him some work experience. No payment. That's how much the guy loves to cook."

Justin crossed his arms tight against his chest. "He's a qualified chef and won lots of awards in Australia. Why does he need more work experience?"

Leah shrugged. "The country club could sponsor him for a working visa."

Justin's eyes nearly bugged out of his head. "What! Does he want to stay? Why?"

Was Justin jealous? She thought he liked Marcus. But obviously, Justin must be angry with him for what had happened.

Leah fiddled with her glittery sleeve. She'd never seen Justin so irritated before. "Marcus is committed to Chris's restaurant back in Australia, but he might consider returning to the US. The country club is a good contact for him and a base where he could come and go." Leah shrugged. "Marcus is the kind of guy who takes one day at a time. He doesn't have any firm plans."

Justin rubbed his chin. "Sounds like you two have gotten close over the last few weeks. You know him well already."

Leah fisted both hips. "Nothing is going on between Marcus and me. He's a friend. I know he's going back to Australia."

Justin raised his hands. "Hey, it's none of my business."

Leah didn't know what to say to that. It should be his business. Maybe this proved she and Justin *were* friends and officially nothing more. Should she explain while she had the opportunity? Would Justin believe her?

"I don't know why you're so upset, Justin. You're the one who wanted me to hang out with Marcus as a façade for my father. Do you know how much trouble it's created for me?"

Justin's jaw flexed. "How much trouble it caused *you?*" The emphasis he placed on his final word was a combination of disbelief and disgust. "I had a meeting with the pastor last week because of what happened. He's not going to let me apply for the youth leader position, thanks to you. The pastor won't say anything to your dad, but he disapproved of our little scheme. I regret the whole thing."

"You and me both. I've been kicked out of home. I've looked for rentals, but everything's too expensive. I have a temporary room at Tabby's B&B but can't stay there forever." Tabby had plans to get the aged bathroom refurbished and redecorated so she could make the room available to guests.

Justin's expression softened. "I'm sorry to hear that. I heard your dad was angry. Are you on speaking terms with him now?"

Leah shook her head violently. "He's a stubborn man. Mom and Dad are furious about me spending time with Marcus. It's wrong how much they judge him. He's actually a decent guy."

Justin rubbed the back of his neck. He opened his mouth and closed it shut.

"Well, I better go." Leah shifted on her feet. "Tabby's waiting for me. Nice talking to you."

He blinked and dropped his hands to his side. "I hope we can put everything behind us and move forward."

Leah raised a brow. "Move forward?"

Justin shook his head. "I mean, be civil to each other."

Leah bit the inside of her cheek. She nodded and offered a polite smile. "Sure. I can be civil. Have a nice night, Justin." She turned away and headed down the hallway to the ladies' restroom. If that wasn't a confirmation that they had no future, then she didn't know what else to think. He'd given up on them all right. Be civil? Boy. It had gotten that bad that he had to ask for basic communication. Sad, indeed.

———

AFTER TAKING a minute to regain his composure, Justin made his way over to his friends. Mumbles of conversation bounced about the ballroom. He spotted Josh and Brandon beside the soda dispensers.

Josh playfully punched Brandon's arm. He stumbled back and knocked into Jodie. She blinked wide eyes at Brandon as her drink spilled over her yellow dress.

Brandon slapped his mouth, but the curl of his lips still showed. That guy always got himself into trouble.

Justin increased his pace. It wasn't his place to save Brandon, but the expression on Jodie's face said her kettle had reached boiling point, and Brandon was about to get scalded.

Josh stood with his arms dangling by his sides but didn't hold back his laughter. He loved to tease his sister.

Justin found a handful of paper napkins and handed them to Jodie. "You look like you could do with some of these."

Jodie's shoulders lowered. "Thank you." She shook her head at Brandon and rolled her eyes. "At least there's one gentleman in the room." Jodie pattered the front of her dress, soaking the napkins in mere seconds.

Justin grabbed another handful and handed them to her.

Brandon scratched his head. "Sorry, Jodie. Let me know if you need me to pay for dry cleaning."

Jodie wiggled her finger in his direction. "You better believe it, buddy. I'll be sending you the bill on Monday."

Josh cupped Brandon's shoulder and pulled him in for a side hug. "Nice work, dude. Way to get back at Jodie."

Jodie glared between her brother and Brandon. "What did I do?"

Her brother tipped his head back, laughed, and pulled his friend away. Justin gave her a hesitant shrug and followed his friends.

He scurried beside Brandon and playfully clipped the side of his head. "Bro, spilling a drink over a girl and insulting her is not how you get her attention."

Brandon jerked his head back. "Who said I was trying to impress Jodie?"

Josh frowned and spat out his words. "Brandon doesn't like Jodie. Not like that."

Justin chewed his lip. Josh must be blind not to notice the love-hate relationship between his sister and Brandon. Justin said no more and kept up with Josh's determined steps. Why was he walking so fast? His usual playful demeanor had soured. They both knew what Brandon was like. Brandon was a player and quite friendly with the single young ladies of Trinity Lakes—not the kind of guy Josh would want to see dating his sister.

Brandon peeked over his shoulder at Justin. "Dare I ask why you took so long in the restroom?" He smirked.

Justin shook his head. "I bumped into Leah in the hallway."

Josh nudged Justin's side. "Back on speaking terms?"

"Barely. It was an intense conversation. Marcus isn't out of the picture. It seems she's spent quite a lot of time with him. But there's nothing I can do about it."

Josh ruffled Justin's hair. "Don't worry. He'll be going back to Australia soon. Then you can have her all to yourself."

His stomach tightened. The idea he was the second choice made him want to hurl.

A group of people passed in front of them, and Leah stood at the fringes of the dance floor, tugging Hannah's arm. Her friend laughed and pulled away. Leah waved to Tabby, but Tabby shook her head.

Most of Leah's friends didn't like to dance, but she enjoyed letting her hair down and having fun. Leah often dragged Justin to the dance floor at social events.

Josh stared at him.

"What?" He raised a palm.

"I can read your mind. You should be on that dance floor with Leah."

Justin took in a deep breath. "I told you we're barely talking."

Brandon punched Justin's arm. "Dude, dancing is dancing. Not talking."

"Ouch! That hurt."

Brandon laughed. "Josh is right. Leah wants you to chase her. Marcus isn't around. Go dance with Leah."

"What are you talking about? She's with her friends and definitely didn't hint she was interested in me five minutes ago."

"You've been avoiding her, so of course she's going to give you the cold shoulder. Be a friend. She needs someone to join her on the dance floor."

The idea was ridiculous, but it might be what Leah and Justin needed to reset their friendship. For some weird reason, his belly went into jittery spasms. His palms broke out in a sweat, and he wiped them down his jeans. Justin took in another long breath and let it release slowly. "Fine, I'll ask her to dance—as friends."

Josh and Brandon shoved each other and guffawed.

Justin ignored them and dug his hands into his back pockets.

Hannah and Tabby noticed him first and faced him, their eyes wide and smiles higher than their hairlines.

Leah stared at her friends then slowly turned in Justin's direction.

He didn't waste a moment and offered his most charming grin. "Looks like your friends don't wanna get down and boogie either." Brandon and Josh wouldn't make so much as a step toward the dance floor.

Justin gestured toward the DJ and a group of friends that moved to the beat. "You want to join me?"

Leah's lips quirked to one side before breaking into a smile, flashing straight teeth. "Sure." She lifted her chin to her friends and scrunched her nose. "Party poopers. Justin and I will show you how it's done." She strode in front of Justin, and he followed behind, capturing her intoxicating perfume.

Her floral dress swished around her knees like a flower on a sunny day. When she spun to face him, her hair brushed her cheek, and a strand stuck to her mouth for a moment. Her lips seemed soft, plump, and inviting. Man, why did this always happen when he got close to her? The last few weeks of agony dissolved when she smiled in his direction. All was right in his world again.

Even though they might never be more than friends, he was glad to be in Leah's company.

They weaved through the crowd a little more and found a space. It wasn't long before Justin found his groove. Leah and he laughed and danced, both in their element. He took her hand, twirled her under his arm, pulled Leah into his chest, and out again. Every time, she fit perfectly there, and her dancing matched his own.

Justin glanced around at his friends of Trinity Lakes and smiled. It had been a while since he'd had the opportunity to dance, and he'd forgotten how good it felt. But when his eyes met Leah's, it all came back so naturally.

She looked beautiful in her floral dress, and her eyes sparkled like the glitter on her thin cardigan.

The DJ's deep voice crackled over the speakers, announcing the next song. It was a slow one, and the entire dance floor seemed to pause for a moment. In the stillness, Leah and he just stood there, their gazes locked.

Something stirred within him, some emotion he couldn't quite identify. If only he could hold her close. But he couldn't. He wasn't sure if this was what she wanted or if she was simply having fun.

Then, as if she had reached a decision, Leah dipped her chin, and when she met his gaze again, there was a shy smile on her face. His heart leaped in his chest. Was this an invitation? Did she want him to ask her to slow dance?

He held his breath and stepped closer. Hesitantly, he placed his hands around her waist, and she responded by placing her hands on his shoulders. For a moment, they stood there, mesmerized. Then the music started, and they swayed to the rhythm. His heart raced with joy as if he was in a dream. He wasn't sure if this dance meant they were back together or not.

She stared past his shoulder, and her eyes went wide. Justin spun around. A waiter stood at the edge of the dance floor, pointing at her.

Leah gestured to herself. "Me?"

The waiter nodded.

Leah stepped around Justin. He followed her movements and joined her.

The man in the black and white suit grinned. "Are you Leah Thompson?"

"Yes, that's me."

He presented a decadent dessert from behind his back. A

white chocolate panna cotta topped with pistachio nuts. "Compliments of the assistant chef."

Justin gulped hard. No. Not now. He couldn't believe the timing.

Leah palmed her cheeks. "Marcus?"

The waiter nodded and handed her the exotic dessert.

Flipping fantastic. Marcus had sideswiped him. Again.

CHAPTER FOURTEEN

Justin rolled out one last strip of black plastic to protect the church carpet from slime. He didn't look forward to cleaning up after tonight's youth games.

The heavy scent of fruity body spray stepped up beside him bringing Kyla with it. "I can finish here. You need to get going and pick up the boys."

Justin would rather drive the minivan and collect the kids any day. He stood to his full height. "Are you sure? You're going to fill the buckets with slime by yourself?"

He bent and scooped a handful of green sludge from a black bucket. The slime dripped through his fingers, leaving a clear sheen in its wake.

Kyla flung a fist into her hip. "If Leah had shown up, she'd be able to help me."

Man. What was with the attitude?

"The pastor said Leah's having a month off." Justin used his shoe to smooth over a bubble in the plastic.

"More like Pastor Dean told her to take a break. Rumors are going around. Someone graffitied her shop last week."

"What?" Justin's jaw flexed. "Who would do such a thing?"

Kyla shrugged. "Probably someone who has no respect for her."

"And no respect for property. That's a shame. No one mentioned her store got damaged. I drive past there every day."

"Tabby came early to paint over it. I might be the only one who saw it."

Justin frowned. If Leah had called him, he would've been there to fix it in a flash. He glanced at his watch. "You're right. I better get going. Thanks for taking over."

The smile she gave him left Justin feeling uneasy. Kyla was the most unusual woman he'd ever met. Something wasn't quite right with her, but he couldn't figure it out.

Ten minutes later, Justin parked the youth van in Tim's driveway. He jogged down the garden path and nearly tripped on the uneven pavers.

The sun was about to disappear, but light still revealed the worn-out state of the house. Paint peeled from the rusty porch swing, and cobwebs filled the corner of the doorframe.

Justin rapped his knuckles on a screen door that had too many ripped holes. He should offer to help Tim's mother fix a few things. Being a single mom, she might not have the funds to pay someone. It had made a significant impact on Justin's mom when the church helped her through some tough times. If it wasn't for that, he might not be serving in a church himself—that initial support changed the direction of his life. That was what drove him to help young people. One little nudge toward the right path could impact their future choices.

Mrs. Winters came to the door and called over her shoulder. "Tim, get your lazy self down here. Your ride is here." She faced Justin. "That kid has been a nightmare this week. He's better behaved after youth group, but it only lasts a day or two." She opened the door. "Come in."

Justin stepped inside. The room smelled musty with a hint of cigarettes. "How are you, Mrs. Winters?"

She waved a hand. "Stop with the formal talk. Call me Annie." Her voice croaked.

"Annie, if you need any odd jobs around the house, you know I'm good with the tools." He patted his imaginary tool belt on his hip.

She smiled wide, revealing stained teeth. "I won't say no. This place is falling apart."

"Maybe I could arrange a few men from the church to come by on Saturday afternoon. You could list the top priorities, and we'll see what we can do."

She touched her throat. "You'd do that?" Her lower eyelids instantly filled with unshed tears.

Justin swallowed the lump in his neck. Times must be tough for Annie.

"I'll make sure it happens." He offered a small smile.

"I appreciate it." She turned over her shoulder again. "Tim, hurry up!" Annie rolled her eyes at Justin. "Why don't you go up there? He might listen to you."

"Sure." Justin passed Annie and took the stairs two steps at a time. He'd been here a few times, so knew which room was Tim's.

The door was open, and Tim was pulling a hoodie over his head.

"Hey, bro. You ready or what?" Justin leaned against the door frame.

Tim peeked from his sweater, his hair spiking in all directions. "What does it look like?"

Justin laughed. "Dude, I'm going to slime you tonight."

Tim laughed. "Not if I get you first."

Justin scanned Tim's messy room. A can of black spray paint caught his eye. "I hope that's not what I think it is" He pointed at the object.

Tim spun to his desk. He rushed over and threw the tin into the trash basket full of chocolate wrappers. "School art project."

When he turned to face Justin, the red in Tim's cheeks showed he was lying.

"Trinity Organics was graffitied last week. Know anything about that?"

Tim lifted his chin and scowled. "No. But I bet she deserved it after what she did to you."

Justin snapped his head back. "Huh? Leah didn't do anything to me. We're friends. We had a little misunderstanding. That's all."

Tim huffed. "You believe in people too easily." He tapped his temple. "You're not street smart."

Justin chuckled. "I don't need to be street smart in little Trinity Lakes. Leah isn't my enemy. She has good qualities"

"See. You're too trusting." Tim waved his hand.

Justin ruffled Tim's hair. "It doesn't hurt to have a little faith in people. I believe in you, my friend. I hope I lead by example, but I make errors too sometimes. As long as we put things right and learn from our mistakes, we grow in maturity." Justin tilted his head. "And if you know who graffitied Leah's shop, can you ask them to apologize to her? She'd forgive them in a blink of an eye."

Tim dipped his chin and met Justin's steady gaze. "I hope you become the youth leader. I'm leaving if Kyla gets the position. That would suck."

Justin palmed Tim's shoulder. "Let's get out of here, or Kyla will have my hide for being late."

———

LAKE WAINSCOTT RIPPLED like a sheet stretched tight as a soft breeze pressed from one bank to the other in a rhythm as old as time. Leah breathed in the fresh air and relaxed her shoulders. Taking a stroll with Marcus was a good way to spend her lunch break.

They followed the cycling path, which sat along the lake's edge. Her Nikes scuffed the paved path, and she took in the tranquil beauty of the lake lapping up on the sandy shore. Main Street was in sight, and the rolling hills of the mountains rose in the distance.

A single figure wearing a worn-out regulation city employee shirt lugged a sack of trash and crouched to collect something from the water's edge. It must be the Junk Man. If it weren't for him, there would be a lot less wildlife … and a lot more trash.

Marcus interrupted her thoughts. "I don't get it. What's the benefit of being a Christian if God didn't protect your shop from vandals? Don't you pray for protection and a blessing over your business? I hear Chris praying about that stuff all the time."

Being around Marcus was refreshing. He asked questions that didn't rattle her faith but made her dig deeper and confirm what she believed.

"It's true that bad things still happen in my life. And I've seen the faith of people in the church when tragedy comes and how they handle it. Just because I've had a setback doesn't mean it wasn't God's will for me to run an organic shop. Anyway, I don't think the vandalism was about someone attacking my faith. It's more likely to be a silly teenager with nothing better to do."

"Do you know why I sent that dessert out to you the other night? It was to cheer you up."

"How did you find out about the graffiti in the first place?"

"I was sorting out a complaint and overheard that Kyla girl talking about it at the next table. She was going on about how sinful it was for the Christians to dance at the party. Then she gossiped about the vandalism on your storefront."

"She's unbelievable."

"I'm sorry I ruined the moment between you and Justin." Marcus stopped in his tracks and faced her.

"What moment?"

"When the waiter returned from the dance floor, he said Justin looked devastated. He said you and Justin were dancing together, and the waiter didn't know what to do with the dessert, but he waved to you, and you dropped everything to take the panna cotta and left the dance floor. Justin apparently looked gobsmacked."

"Really?" Leah covered her mouth. "I can't believe I just left him there. I did do that. How terrible."

"He must be jealous."

"Of who?"

Marcus chuckled and pretended to flex his muscles. "Of me. Why wouldn't he be? I am competition, but he probably doesn't understand that we're friends, and that's all we will ever be."

Leah blinked. She only saw him as a friend too, but to hear Marcus speak it directly like that surprised her. Why did it surprise her?

"Justin has nothing to worry about now. I'm heading back to Australia soon, but I want to visit again sometime." Marcus resumed walking.

Leah skipped a step to catch up. "Can't you extend your visa and work at the country club?" she asked.

"No. Chris needs me, and it's too much short notice. I don't want to do that to him, even though he said I'm more than welcome. Plus, it's a bit complicated. I have to return to Australia, apply for a working visa from there, and plan every-thing. Maybe I will some other time. For now, I'm helping Chris establish the second restaurant."

"It's great that you're committed to him. You have a good work ethic, Marcus."

"Thanks. I've been thinking about you and Justin. I can see why he went to desperate measures to date you. He is a man in love and desperate to do whatever it takes to win his woman."

Leah laughed. "His woman?"

"That's how some blokes talk in Australia. Sorry—you're not

a possession. I hope it didn't sound like that. I'm not good with romance talk. But you get what I mean. Justin wants you to be his special lady." He shrugged. "Since he's a strong believer, I assume he wants something permanent, like marriage."

Leah frowned. "Don't you want a wife one day?"

Marcus twisted his lips like he'd chewed sour candy. "I'm too young to think about that. I'm establishing my career first. I have more awards to win before I marry and start a family."

So she was right. Marcus was career focused. Not that she took Marcus as a potential anything. It had been more than two months since her disastrous date with Marcus, and she wasn't over having feelings for Justin.

"Are you going to forgive Justin and take him back? Aren't Christians supposed to forgive?"

"It's not that simple."

"I'm a simple guy, and I can't see why that wouldn't work. Why complicate it?"

Marcus had a point. Of course, if Justin had done something terrible or harmful, she still would have to forgive him. That didn't mean having to accept him back or associate with him, but what he had done was repairable. Marcus was likely right— Justin did it all out of desperation to be with her. They had both learned it wasn't the best strategy, but there was nothing immoral in their desire to be together as a couple.

"Thanks, Marcus. It's been good to get a man's view."

"Does that mean you'll give him a second chance?"

Leah picked at her chipped nail polish. "It's whether he will give *me* a second chance—that's the question."

CHAPTER FIFTEEN

Tabby cleared the plates from that morning's guests. Leah held up a hand before she took her cereal bowl. She leaned her chest against the table and whispered, "I get a discounted rate. You've got to stop trying to clean up after me. The least I can do is wash my dishes."

Tabby shook her head and whispered back, "I have a machine for that. It's called a dishwasher."

"I can stack it for you. How about that?" Leah pushed back her padded chair and collected their coffee mugs. She passed the window featuring the wrap-around veranda that looked out over the property's sweeping grounds, flanked by a flourishing lawn and immaculate gardens.

Leah followed Tabby into the whitewashed wooden country kitchen and placed the cups beside the stainless-steel sink. A plum tree stood outside the white-framed window, boasting of its abundant fruit. The freshly painted walls did brighten up the place. Sage-green had sounded sickly when Tabby had first mentioned it, but it made a perfect backdrop for the wooden shelves displaying beautiful bone china cup and saucer sets and matching plates.

Leah unstacked the clean cutlery from the dishwasher, humming a worship song that remained stuck in her mind from her devotional time.

Tabby tilted her head. "I got a call from the cabinet makers this morning. They pushed the job forward and can renovate Gran's en suite. They start today."

Leah straightened. "The en suite attached to the room I'm staying in?"

Tabby placed her hands on her hips and smirked. "That'll be the one."

"And which cabinet makers are you getting in?"

"The only business in town that makes cabinets."

"Where Justin works?"

"I can see how you graduated top of the class." Tabby tapped her temple. "You're a smart cookie."

"You guys love to bring that up." Leah rolled her eyes and looked heavenward.

A rumble of an engine came from outside. Leah craned her neck toward the window. Mac, Nick, and David jumped out of the truck.

"That'll be Justin and the team now. They mustn't have read my email about coming after nine. Oh well. Guests have finished breakfast early so it'll be fine."

Leah's heart skipped a beat when Justin hopped out of the vehicle. She stood back before he saw her gawking. She chewed on her fingernails. Why was she so nervous?

Tabby scrunched her brows. "You and Justin are on speaking terms, even danced together not that long ago. I didn't think it would be a problem."

"It's not a problem at all." Leah and Justin might be on speaking terms with each other, but deeper feelings still simmered underneath the surface. She should be satisfied with friendship status and not expect any more from him. They still hadn't had a proper conversation about the picnic disaster.

Tabby pointed to the dirty dishes beside the sink. "Can I take you up on your offer to start the dishwasher? I'll greet the men and show them to the bathroom." She pitter-patted her hands in front of her chest. "I'm excited to see the renovation."

Leah's stomach dipped and turned. Staying at the B&B wasn't convenient now, with tradesmen walking in and out of her room all day, leaving their trail. And not having the bathroom in full operation wasn't ideal.

Leah forced a grin. "I'll stack the dishwasher and clean up a little, but I better head upstairs and make sure I haven't left any underwear on my bed or something." Sure, it would be embarrassing if she'd left lace panties lying around, but all she owned were underpants with moth holes and stretched elastic overdue to be thrown out. Now her debts were nearly paid, she should do something about that. A whole new wardrobe would be nice.

Tabby chuckled. "Good idea. See you up there."

Leah worked at sonic speed, tidying the kitchen while the tradesmen unloaded, and she managed to scurry up the stairs with thirty seconds to spare. Just as she'd expected, her full briefs dangled over a laundry basket. She collected a used towel from the bathroom and shoved it into the basket to cover her personal items.

Mumbled voices and heavy footsteps came closer to the bedroom. Leah spun around and swung her hands behind her back. Heat flashed across her cheeks. Why was she so embarrassed about her granny underwear? She was staying in the granny suite.

One of Justin's colleagues carried the front of a long, slender cardboard box. Justin held the back end firmly in his palms.

He looked up in surprise and smiled. "Hey, Leah. How are you doing?"

Her mouth went dry as she nodded. Crackled words came from her tongue. "Good, thank you." Why was she so awkward? Maybe the unsaid words after the dance they'd shared still hung in limbo. She had feelings for him yet wasn't sure of where she stood in terms of their relationship. The men moved past her into the ensuite.

Tabby entered the room. "Sorry. This is gonna be a pain in the backside for you." She pouted in a frown. "You can bunk in my room for the week. Your call."

Justin poked his head into the bedroom, concern lining his brow, then disappeared into the ensuite.

Leah turned to Tabby. "I need to move out of here anyway. You'll need to rent this room at full price once it's ready. Leah scanned the worn carpet, aged floral wallpaper, and clashing curtains. Tabby had plans to renovate, redecorate, and remove any trace of the 1980s. The writing was on the wall—Leah needed to find another place to live. And quick.

"I haven't found any reasonable accommodation in my budget." Leah rubbed her forehead. "I might need to suck up to Mom and Dad with my tail between my legs and apologize." Although she hadn't done anything knowingly wrong. She let out a heavy sigh. All she'd done was pretend to date Marcus— that part had been deceiving.

Justin returned to the bedroom and rested a palm on Leah's shoulder. "Are you going to be okay? Is there anything I can do to help?"

Leah managed a small smile. "Listening to our conversation, were you?"

"The space isn't that large." He smiled and dropped his hand.

Workers moved past them and back down the stairs. Tabby gave Leah a look that said here's-your-chance-to-talk moment and followed the workers out of the room.

"I don't know how you can help. I feel like I'm going backward by returning home." Leah met Justin's kind eyes. "Dad should be the one to apologize for how he yelled at me and how controlling he was."

"He has been known to apologize on rare occasions." Justin raised his eyebrows.

"I could be waiting for years. Is suffering his silent treatment worth it? I'm hesitant to face his reaction. I don't know if he's calmed down enough to take me back."

"I think he has. And you won't know unless you try."

"Anyway, I shouldn't be living with my parents at this stage. What do you think?" She studied the worn ruby carpet, which would be ripped up soon enough.

Justin's eyes went wide. "My opinion?" He shifted on his feet. "Your dad is a stern man, that's for sure, but nothing you do or say will change his personality. If I had a beautiful daughter …" He tipped her chin to meet his gaze. "I guess I'd be a little over-protective too."

He shrugged. "Your dad cares about you and wants the best for you." Justin directed his gaze to the window for a beat.

Did Justin think he wasn't the best for her? He wasn't second best. He came in first place.

Justin turned back to face her and raked his fingers through his hair. "You can only ask him and see what he says. Don't go with any expectations. Then you won't be disappointed."

Leah ran a hand down her cheek. "I'm already disappointed that he's upset with me. I've spent my life being the good girl to avoid his disapproval. I don't like seeing him upset. But I can't live at home and be the dutiful daughter forever." Leah pinched the bridge of her nose. "I don't have much of a choice. I need more time to find some real estate."

Justin took her hand, and Leah blinked. "Shall we pray about it before you go?"

Leah glanced at their joined hands. "I need all the prayer I can get." She studied his sincere gaze. "Thank you."

Justin smiled and squeezed her hand. They prayed together, but at the sound of returning footsteps, Justin ended the prayer quickly and stepped away from Leah. "Give me a call if you need anything else. If things don't go well with your dad, I'll find a place for you to stay."

Leah nodded, slowly coming out of a daze. "I better get going and open the shop. See you around town."

Justin's grin broadened. "Will do."

———

LEAH STOOD behind the counter at Trinity Organics, crossing off the tasks she had completed that day. The shop was nearly empty after a rush of customers in the morning. Another influx of clients would come in at lunch.

Ellie Reilly approached not seeming as chirpy as usual. Had her mom taken a bad turn?

"Hey Ellie. How's your mom doing lately?" It was no secret Mrs. Reilly struggled with fatigue.

"She's the reason I'm here. I read somewhere that bone broth has a lot of health benefits. Does your chicken soup use bone broth as a base?"

"It does. I have some left from this morning's batch."

Ellie smiled. "Great. Don't tell Jackson. My brother is convinced that anything the slightest bit alternative is weird."

"Which seems ironic, considering he's working on a ranch." Leah laughed. "You'd think he'd avoid processed foods."

"Right? But then he's so busy working that he barely notices what he eats. If he keeps this up, I won't be getting bone broth just for my mom, but him as well." She winked. "I'll need to find a way to hide it in his chocolate milkshakes or something."

Leah scrunched her nose. That would taste awful and turn Jackson right away from alternative remedies. "I'll get you some for your mom then. Won't be a minute."

She prepared the order and took payment from Ellie. "Message me if you need more as it sells out quickly."

Ellie nodded. "Thanks for this. I'm sure I'll be back soon." She headed to the front door just as it swung open.

In strolled Tim, one of the teens from youth group. He was dressed in a faded T-shirt and jeans, his hands stuffed in his pockets. His eyes shifted this way and that as he trailed a finger along the tubs of nuts and dried fruit.

"Yo, Leah." Tim lifted his chin in her direction, a nervous smile dancing across his lips. "What's up?"

Leah raised her brows. "Not much," she called back to him. "What can I do for you?"

Tim seemed taken aback by the question. He nervously jingled the change in his pocket as he approached her. "Um—" He stopped short and fiddled with his cap, switching it forward and backward. His Adam's apple slid up and down his throat before he finally spoke. "I came to apologize."

Leah's eyes narrowed. "Apologize? What for?"

Tim dipped his gaze to the floor. "It was me who graffitied your shop." His voice came out low and laced with shame.

A flood of anger washed over her. "Why?" She was careful not to expose her emotions. It was good that he was coming to her with the truth, but she was still furious.

"I don't know." Tim shook his head. "I was angry about what you did to Justin, and it was the first thing that came to mind." He gave her a puppy-eyed plea. "I'm sorry. I'll do anything to make it up to you. Pay for the paint. Clean. Anything."

Leah came around the counter and stood before him. She crossed her arms over her chest. "That was a terrible thing to say about me, and to scrawl it over my shopfront could ruin my reputation and affect my livelihood. It's a very serious offense." She could hear her dad's voice in her head. This was how he dealt with teens. He didn't dismiss the crime too easily. But she also wanted to show grace.

Tim blinked. "I didn't think about that."

Leah placed a gentle hand on his shoulder. "No. You

wouldn't have. That's why it's better not to react to situations. Allow time to think things through and get all the facts. Then respond the right way."

Tim nodded slowly, like he was actually taking in her words. "Yeah. I could avoid getting into a lot of trouble at school if I tried that. Makes sense."

Leah smiled and dropped her hand. "Good. Glad you're willing to listen." She playfully tapped her chin. "Now, what can I get you to do to make up for it?" She looked to the ceiling and dramatically raised a finger in the air. "I know. You can be my guinea pig and taste test some of my healthy food."

Tim wrinkled his nose. "Should I wear a bell around my neck too?"

Leah tilted her head back and laughed hard. "You don't need a bell. Making you eat healthy food is the perfect thing to improve my day."

"Whatever you need to get your kicks." He shrugged. "Sure, I can eat vegetables."

Leah walked past him to the fermented food section. Oh, she'd love to make him eat sauerkraut or kimchi. But no, she should surprise him with something nice. She wanted him to learn that eating healthy could taste good.

In one of the cane baskets, fresh figs with purple skin grabbed her attention. Argh. She could have fun with this. She scooped one into her hand and faced Tim. "Right. You need to eat one of these."

He tilted his head with a look of confusion. "That's all?"

"Yep." She suppressed an evil cackle as she punctured the skin and tore the fruit in half, revealing stringy flesh.

"Ew!" Tim jumped back. "It has maggots."

Leah jiggled the fig under his nose. "You have to eat it." She couldn't stop the smile playing with her lips. Oh, teenagers were fun to tease. This was what she missed out on in having a younger sibling. Just for a moment, she'd enjoy this.

"Are you crazy? I'm not eating that." He held up a cross sign and cowered to the side.

Leah stepped into his space. "Come on. Don't look at it. Just throw it in your mouth, chew, and swallow. You can do it. I believe in you, Tim." This time she couldn't help but laugh.

Tim gave her a you're-a-weirdo look.

Leah dropped her arms to her side. "I'll eat one first. How's that?"

Tim straightened and crossed his arms. "I'd like to see this."

She held her head back and popped the fig into her mouth. "Mmm." She chewed around her words. "Simply divine."

When she lowered her chin and met his eyes, pure awe covered Tim's expression. He pumped his fist to his chest. "Respect."

Leah laughed. "Okay. Your turn." She skipped to the basket and plucked another fig, offering it to him as though she was the witch from Snow White holding the poisoned apple. "Eat, my pretty."

Tim smiled this time and hesitantly took the fig. "I hope this one doesn't have maggots." He eyed the fruit cautiously.

Should she tell him? Nah. This was too much fun.

He squinted at her, swiftly shoved it into his mouth, and chewed vigorously. His eyes went wide for a bit, then he slowed his pace and scrunched his brows. "This actually tastes all right." He finished chewing and swallowed. "Kinda mushy and sweet. Not bad. Can I have another one?"

"God's candy. Fresh figs are my favorite." She smiled. "Sure, you can have more. I'll give you some to take home to your mom."

———

AFTER WORK THAT DAY, Leah's hands shook the whole way to her childhood home. Why was she so fearful of Dad's reaction?

Should she come back under his control? She couldn't legally set up a bed and sleep in her warehouse. In this gossipy town, someone would find out somehow, and Dad would arrest her. She laughed at the irony.

Leah hopped out of her Ford and practically tiptoed up the path toward her parents' home. She rapped the door with her knuckles and took a deep breath.

Dad's voice mumbled. "I'll get it."

Bother. She'd hoped Mom would be the first to see her, so she could help soften the blow. Instead, Leah needed to grin and bear it and face her father.

The door swung open. Dad's eyes bulged. "Leah?" The word didn't come out angry. Maybe he had missed her.

"Dad, how are you?"

He crossed his arms over his broad chest covered by his uniform. "I'm good. What's going on? Why are you here?"

Okay, so Dad hadn't missed her. Leah dug her hands into the pockets of her jeans. "I've come to apologize for my part in how things …" Why did she feel so intimidated when her dad was growly? Leah scratched the back of her head. "I want to explain myself."

Dad lowered his brows. "Go on."

"In Australia, cider means something else. It's an alcoholic drink, and I wasn't aware that I was drinking alcohol. It tasted more fermented than usual, but I assumed it was because of the type of fruit used. I didn't think about it much. We were eating food."

Dad's bottom lip rolled outward as if his tongue ran over his teeth.

"Dad, I haven't taken up drinking. I had a terrible headache the next day, and I'm sorry for being disrespectful in how I spoke." She swallowed hard.

Dad nodded, still not saying a word.

"And Marcus is heading back to Australia. Soon. There's nothing romantic going on between us."

Dad dropped his hands to his sides and let out a loud exhale. "Thank the Lord. You can do a lot better than him."

Leah's stomach tightened. She didn't appreciate the way Dad spoke about Marcus. She valued his friendship, and she valued him as a person. Should she stick up for Marcus, or would that cause more angst?

Justin's earlier conversation came back to her mind. Dad wouldn't likely change his opinion easily about anything. He was the type of man who remained set in his ways.

Leah bit the inside of her cheek, holding her breath momentarily. How should she respond?

Dad let go of a grin and opened his arms wide. "It's like the prodigal son story." He chuckled. "Welcome home, my daughter." He stepped forward and wrapped his arms around her.

She stiffened. Dad changed his attitude as soon as he discovered she and Marcus weren't a thing. But what if she dated someone else he didn't approve of?

Like Justin?

Dad squeezed harder, and she automatically hugged him back. Did he assume she was moving back in before she had a chance to ask? What did that say about her? Dad believed she needed to rely on them, as if she wasn't ready for independence. Her mind became muddled. Although she needed to come home now, she would make it her mission to find somewhere else to live. And soon.

CHAPTER SIXTEEN

Justin placed the hand sander on the bench and ran his fingers over the oak, admiring the dark and red tones and fine grain. He massaged a spot in the crook of his palm where a cramp had formed from his vigorous sanding. He enjoyed working on carpentry, but most of the jobs that came through were basic cabinets. His favorite project of all time was a kitchen they'd made for Susannah Gilbertson, Hannah's mother. She could afford to have the best wood imported. The kitchen became a work of art. All that was during his apprenticeship years ago, and his boss had been super stressed, watching over Justin's shoulder, making sure everything was perfect.

Wood shavings littered the floor. The woodshop had a musky aroma, a mix of metal tools, sawdust, and staining oil.

"Yoo-hoo!" A distinctive voice echoed about the warehouse, a voice which could only belong to one person—Rhonda Ingalls. She was an interesting woman. That was a kind way of putting it. Justin wiped his hands on his overalls and strode to the showroom.

Rhonda barreled toward him with a look of determination on her face.

Justin held up a hand. "Don't cross into the safety area, please, Mrs. Ingalls. Let me come to you." His work boots squeaked on the concrete as he rushed his steps. "How can I help you, ma'am?"

"Hope you have a minute to spare. I happened to be passing by the area." She fluttered a hand above her head, tilting her body to the side.

Just passing by. Sure.

"And I remembered some important information I was sure you'd find very exciting."

"Is that so?" Justin rubbed his temple. Strange how the ache in his lower back had immediately transferred to his head from one interaction with Rhonda Ingalls.

"This is top secret." Rhonda looked left and right. "Kyla is changing churches."

No one could overhear the conversation with all the machinery going on out the back.

Justin tapped his chin. "Top secret, but I'm allowed to know?"

"It's good news for you." Rhonda palmed the air like his question was juvenile. "Now you don't have any competition for the youth leader role."

Justin shook his head. "It's not a competition, Mrs. Ingalls."

She tsked. "Yes, dear, I know that, but Kyla was determined to be the top dog." Rhonda slapped her mouth. "That didn't come out right. I mean … after the fiasco with Caleb and their broken engagement, it appears she wants to start over. Pastor Dean hasn't opened the position to her, even though she's hinted at her interest several times." She tapped the side of her nose. "But I have inside information that she wasn't a likely candidate anyway. The pastor must've had words with her, because she left." Rhonda lifted her hands in a shrug. "Now you've moved into first place."

There was no way he would tell the gossip queen that he'd had a conversation with Pastor Dean too. He must believe that Kyla wasn't ready either.

"I need more time to work on myself before I can lead others."

Rhonda frowned. "Dear boy, don't let your past dictate your future. I know some elders in the church still hold your wild teenage days against you, but that isn't fair."

Her words were like a bullet to his chest. Some elders would vote against him. Just like the sheriff, they held his past mistakes against him. And likely, some associated him with his father's reputation, although they wouldn't outwardly use that as a reason. Justin clenched and released his fists. Justin understood his new identity in Christ. He was not responsible for his dad's mistakes.

He opened his mouth to speak, but he must be wise with the likes of Rhonda Ingalls. He slammed his mouth shut and waited for her to say more. Rhonda always had more to say. The woman used a lot of words.

"My husband is on the board of elders, although he doesn't tell me everything. After quite a bit of prodding and nudges, I read between the lines." Her grin grew. "I'm not one hundred percent certain of what was said, but we can be sure Kyla has moved on." She patted his cheek. "I'm in your corner, young man. When the position opens for applications, Mr. Ingalls fully supports you running the youth group. So do others. Don't let the little incident with Leah hold you back."

Justin ground his back teeth. Was Mrs. Ingalls insinuating that a relationship with Leah would affect his reputation? He had made the mistake of thinking that himself, but that would make him as judgmental as the people who held his past against him. He needed to ask Leah what exactly had happened. Had she truly been rolling in the grass with Marcus? No one else had reported them being affectionate in public. But surely Leah wouldn't have danced with Justin if her heart was set on Marcus. Unless she was confused about who to choose. Justin wanted Leah to pick him for himself, not because Marcus was leaving.

"Mrs. Ingalls, thank you for your support and belief in me." Justin ran his teeth over his bottom lip. He couldn't say anything else, or the good gossipers of Trinity Lakes could and would use it against him. "I need to get back to work. We have a lot of jobs lined up. I'll see you at church on Sunday."

Rhonda leaned forward and cupped his cheek in a motherly gesture. "Wonderful. Now, remember what I said about applying for the position. It's a sure thing."

The woman had no idea.

———

AFTER TWO WEEKS of living back at home, Leah still hadn't unpacked all her boxes. This was temporary. Leah smoothed the wrinkles out of her cream-colored quilt cover displaying sunflowers and green leaves, a gift from her mother. She puffed the matching pillow and placed it lightly against the corduroy headrest.

Light coming in from the window flickered against her dresser. The sun's rays illuminated the folds of the drapes. Each of them caught the light differently, creating a powerful 3D effect and mesmerizing her deeper into her melancholy thoughts.

She shook her head and picked up her daily devotional. Leah scanned the words for some encouragement. Dad hadn't apologized for anything, and she wouldn't be getting an apology from him in this lifetime. Leah opened her Bible app next and typed in the search bar, "honor parents." How did that work now that she was an adult? How did Tim from the Bible correct an elderly man? She searched for that scripture and prayed about the situation before heading downstairs for breakfast.

Leah's feet padded over the cold tiles as she entered the kitchen.

Dad looked up from his newspaper and smiled. "Morning, princess." He held a cup of coffee in his right hand, and the newspaper in his left. "What plans do you have for this Saturday?"

Leah removed a pitcher of orange juice from the fridge and a glass from the cabinet. After she poured herself a drink, she joined her dad at the table. "I have the morning off. Nina is filling in for me today." Leah rested her forehead into her palm.

The rustle of newspaper and Dad's palm on the table made her look up.

Dad scratched at his temple. The hair had grayed on the sides but remained dark brown on top. "You seem a little depressed. Is that why you have the morning off?"

Leah took a deep breath and exhaled slowly. She was feeling flat this morning.

Dad touched her arm. "Is this about Marcus? I heard he's going back to Australia today. Did you fall in love with him?"

Leah nibbled on her top lip. Should she challenge Dad's attitude toward Marcus? After reading this morning's scriptures, Leah mustered self-control and chose her words carefully. Would she be able to carry on a conversation without getting upset?

"I miss Marcus, but as a friend. I've only loved one man—Justin. I still care for him, but you disapprove. It's hard for me to choose between honoring you and following my heart."

Dad's lips flatlined. "A parent isn't emotionally involved. We can see things our children wouldn't notice. That's why I discouraged you from pursuing a relationship with Justin."

Leah straightened. Irritation zinged up her spine. "Dad, can't you see that I'm not a child anymore? I need to learn to make my own decisions, which may mean making mistakes. I value your opinion and insight, but I need to learn to pray and hear from God myself and work it out. Discern what comes from my emotions and what's right to do."

A slow smile crept up Dad's cheeks. "You have grown up, and I can see that you can make decisions. It's hard for me to let go, especially since you're our only child. Besides, I like having you living under our roof. That makes me want to protect you more. It's in my DNA to protect people. Heck, it's why I became a sheriff."

Leah rubbed her dad's forearm. "I appreciate your heart and how you want the best for me. I do feel protected. Sometimes it's a little too much and—" She chose not to say "smothering" and closed her mouth.

Dad nodded and must've got her point.

"Can you trust me to decide whether Justin is right for me?"

Dad scratched the back of his head. "Justin and I have made amends. I've already told him I was wrong and approved of him pursuing you."

Leah bolted upright, and her chair fell to the floor. She placed her hands on her hips. "What? When did this happen? You approve of Justin?"

Dad chuckled. "When I thought you might run off with an Australian and leave the country, I panicked and asked Justin to go after you."

Leah paced up and down the kitchen floor. She paused and faced her father. "But he didn't. Why not? Why hasn't Justin told me you're okay with us being together?" She raised her palms.

Dad got out of his chair and hugged her shoulders. "Probably because you were dating another man. He wanted you to choose him."

Leah turned into her father's embrace, and a tear trickled

down her cheek, seeping into his shirt. "I would always choose Justin. Doesn't he know that?"

Dad hugged her tighter and stroked Leah's hair. "Men need clear communication. You need to tell him. Obviously, he doesn't know, or he'd be on our doorstep to take you on a date. That guy is crazy in love with you."

Leah pulled back and peeked up at her dad. "You can see it?"

He laughed. "The whole town knows. He's had his eye on you for years."

Leah swiped a tear from under her eye and released a laugh. "He's a real sweetheart. I love him."

"If you're sure about Justin and have peace about the relationship, tell him how you feel."

Leah frowned. "Shouldn't the guy pursue the girl?"

He offered a reassuring smile. "Justin has chased you for a long time. I've been a big roadblock. Now I'm stepping out of the way. Why don't you find him and tell him how you feel? Make sure he knows you didn't like Marcus romantically."

Leah covered her mouth. "I didn't intend to hurt Justin. I thought he didn't want a relationship with me anymore. And he was only being nice as a friend."

"He's been in love with you for the past five years. One mistake won't erase his feelings for you."

Hope rose in Leah's chest. Her feelings for him hadn't disappeared when they last talked. "You're right." Dad wasn't right about everything, but he did have wisdom she could learn from. "When I see Justin next, I'll talk things through."

CHAPTER SEVENTEEN

W hy did Pastor Dean make Justin take the Australians to the airport? He guessed it was because he drove the old minivan the most. Chris Evanson, the head chef, sat in the passenger seat. Marcus's bulky body filled up the spot behind Chris.

Justin crunched the stick into second as he rounded the corner.

"Sounds like the gearbox needs some TLC." Chris smiled, but his expression flatlined. "Is everything okay?"

Justin internally groaned. He must've had a scowl on his face. "Yeah, good. Just tired." Justin forced a grin. "Don't worry. I'm alert enough to drive properly."

Chris smirked and squinted at the same time. "Don't have lady troubles, do you? I've seen that look in my kitchen—when a staff member can't shake it off, it consumes their mind."

The rumble of the engine covered up their conversation from the people in the back seats. Chris looked like the pastoral type. They were in for a long trip to Tri-Cities Airport, and Justin had time to open up. Marcus was in close hearing range, so Justin lowered his voice. "Did you hear about the fake picnic date that went wrong?"

"I heard it went bad for Leah. Poor girl mistakes cider for a soft drink, trips over, and falls onto Marcus right when some woman happens to be spying on them. Of all people, the sheriff's daughter gets caught in the wrong moment and gets kicked out of the house. Terrible."

Justin gripped the steering wheel tighter. "That's not how it happened."

Marcus draped his arms over Chris's headrest. "Yeah, that's how it happened, all right. I was there, mate. What's your version of the story?"

Justin rolled his eyes. He hadn't been talking quietly enough. Was Marcus telling the truth? "I heard it from Rhonda, the lady who caught you guys rolling in the grass." Justin ground his teeth. The thought of it made his blood boil.

"She's wrong. Leah isn't that kind of girl. And believe it or not, I'm not that kind of guy. I didn't realize what you call cider is the non-alcoholic drink we call sparking apple juice. Our cider is called hard cider in the US."

Mmm. That sounded like a convenient excuse.

"I also didn't realize Leah wouldn't want to drink alcohol at all. So I didn't say anything when she asked for the organic cider —hard cider. No wonder it affected her so much, if she's not used to drinking—"

That much was true. Justin wasn't a drinker either. Never had been.

"—and she drank too much too fast. She fell. Gossip Lady ran off without waiting for an explanation. Leah thought it was funny at the time, but that was just the effects of the cider. And that made her bold enough to stand up to her dad. He was furious, but he didn't listen either. I can't believe you thought badly of her all this time. Is that why you've been giving her the cold shoulder?"

Justin couldn't believe what he was hearing. "I thought she was pulling back because she was dating you for real. You asked me for permission."

"I was testing to see how serious you were about her. You seemed to give up pretty easily. I tried to make you jealous by asking what you'd think if I dated her, and I was shocked that you didn't react. Seemed to me you weren't that invested in her in the first place."

"What was I supposed to do? I thought she kissed another guy. That's not the kind of woman I want to be with. I want someone who wants me and no one else."

Marcus raised his hand. "I could tell she wasn't into me, one hundred percent. She talked about you a lot, but she was angry that you'd judged her—like her dad and other people."

"Oh, man. This makes much more sense."

Chris palmed Justin's shoulder. "Looks like you've got some apologizing to do when you return to Trinity Lakes."

"I'll need to get down on my knees and grovel."

"It's a long trip home. Plenty of time to come up with your take-me-back speech." Chris chuckled, and Marcus followed.

Laughter bubbled up in Justin's belly, and he joined the men. It was the first time he could laugh since the picnic date. What a relief to know he'd misunderstood the situation and Leah hadn't changed.

If Leah hadn't changed, maybe she still cared.

———

AFTER JUSTIN DROPPED the Australians at the airport, the first thing he did when he was back on the highway was call Leah.

She answered on the fourth ring. "Hi, Justin. how are you?" She sounded happy to hear from him.

"I'm good. Real good. Hey, I'll be passing through Walla Walla in a couple of hours and wondered if you had any orders or anything you need me to pick up for your shop while I'm there."

"Oh. That's nice of you to think of me. I do have one order that's scheduled to be delivered on Monday. It would save me the shipping costs if you picked it up."

"Great. Text me the details. I'll go get it now and meet you at Trinity Organics."

"Oh, I have the day off, but Nina is there."

Justin tapped his steering wheel. What excuse did he have to meet up with her?

"I guess I could meet you down there and help unload," Leah said. "Text me when you're close to town."

"Awesome. See you then." Hope rose in his chest. Now he had to figure out the right words to say.

Later that morning, Justin parked at the Organic Collective wholesalers. He didn't have a high visibility safety vest. He searched for the contact number on his phone and called the owner. "Hey, Daniel. I'm here to pick up the Trinity Organics order. I can't come inside because I don't have a hi-vis vest. Would you be able to bring the produce to my van?"

"There's a spare vest on a hook inside the door. Put that on and head down the back. I'm still packing the order as Leah originally didn't want it until Monday."

"I was in the area. Thanks for accommodating us. See you in a minute." Justin strode to the entrance and slipped on the fluorescent orange vest. Forklifts beeped and swiveled around the warehouse, lifting crates to and from the blue pallet racking. Justin stayed out of their way and followed the yellow lines on the concrete floor.

Daniel bent over at the waist, glanced up, and smiled. "Haven't seen you around for a while."

Justin had occasionally made pick-ups when he was near Walla Walla, but he'd stopped doing favors for Leah more than a month ago. "Yep. I'm back."

"Glad to hear it. I got a little worried when Leah turned up with a handsome young man from Australia. I had an eerie feeling she might run off with him and set up business Down Under. The guy knew a lot about the industry. He sounds like the ambitious type."

Justin's mouth dried in an instant. He had those same thoughts. He cleared his throat. "That won't happen on my watch."

"That's a relief." Daniel added two boxes to the pallet and checked off his list.

"Can I help you with anything?"

Daniel pointed to the darkened corner on the other side of the room. "You can use that trolley over there and grab two sacks of potatoes for me. Don't break your back doing it."

"Don't worry. I'm well-trained in safety procedures. I know how to lift correctly." He had learned the hard way when he was an apprentice. He'd twisted his lower back and couldn't walk for a week.

Justin made his way over, and a line of ceramic coolers caught his eye. They each stood on a wrought iron stand. The one with the blue and purple glaze had a painting of a windmill and landscape. Leah would love one of those.

He turned over his shoulder. "How much for a water cooler?"

Daniel straightened and made his way over. "They aren't just any water dispenser. They're pieces of art. Each one is hand-crafted, They have a Royal Doulton filter inside, which removes fluoride, chlorine, and any nasty chemicals."

Justin ran his finger on the cool surface. "I'd like to buy Leah one for her shop."

"I can give you the wholesale price—one hundred and eighty dollars, plus the filter, which lasts twelve months."

Justin didn't even blink at the price. Leah probably wouldn't spend that amount on herself with her tight budget. "Can you put it on a separate order? I'll pay cash."

"That blue one is my favorite too. Last time Leah was here, she was looking at that one in particular." Daniel found its packing box and carefully placed the purifier and scrunched paper inside.

Justin rolled two burlap bags of potatoes onto a trolley and delivered them to the pallet. Daniel finalized the order, and Justin got back on the road.

An hour later, he parked next to Trinity Organics' back door. He texted Leah that he had arrived, then reversed the minivan to the roller door and lifted the trunk. Boxes and crates were pressed against the metal luggage barrier behind the back seats.

The cranking of the roller door had Justin turning to witness the most beautiful sight in town—Leah Thompson. He couldn't stop his broad smile. She was a breath of fresh air, and now he had cleared his mind of prejudices and misunderstandings, he could allow himself to fall deeper in love with her.

He leaned his back on the van and crossed his ankles. "You're looking gorgeous as always."

Leah glanced at her outfit, seeming a little surprised. "Um. Thanks." She fiddled with her necklace. "Oh, I can get you a trolley for that." She turned, and twenty seconds later, she pushed a red trolley toward him. "Thank you for collecting the order."

He took the handle from her, and their fingers brushed. "My pleasure. I was in the area, dropping Chris, Marcus, and their team at the airport."

"Yeah. I heard you were taking them. I said my goodbyes yesterday."

He smiled. "I got you a little something while at the whole-salers." He turned his back, retrieved the first box, and carefully lowered it to the ground. No markings were on the cardboard. He reached into his pocket, used the keys to slice the tape, and opened the lid. "I couldn't wait to give this to you." He stood back and gestured to the box. "Take a peek."

Leah stared at him and tentatively approached the gift. "I think I know what this is." She met his gaze and gave him a beautiful smile. "Why did you get this for me?"

"I wanted to. And it's my 'I'm sorry' offering."

She raised a brow before pulling out two mounds of butcher paper. Her head snapped up. "Oh, you got the blue one. Did Daniel tell you this was the one I wanted?"

"I picked it out first, but yes, he mentioned you seemed to like that one the most."

Leah lowered the lid back on the purifier and approached Justin. "This is very thoughtful of you." She tilted her head. "What do you mean by 'I'm sorry?' What are you apologizing for?"

He took her hand in his. "Sorry for being a big jerk. The fake date was a big mistake. I should've taken your advice and tried to get to know your dad. I'm also sorry for not talking things through with you after Rhonda told me what happened. I withdrew, not wanting to clarify the truth, and believed Rhonda's version of the story. Marcus and Chris told me what actually happened. I'm sorry for believing the gossip. Can we go back to where we started? Do things the right way."

Leah took his other hand and squeezed. "Sounds good to me."

"Really?" Joy exploded in his chest.

"Yes. Really. Dad isn't going to stand in our way anymore. He likes you now. But even if he didn't, I need to trust my heart. We're right for each other."

Justin wrapped his arms around her waist and pulled Leah into his chest. "I believe that too." He kissed the top of her head and inched back, not letting her go. "I missed you."

Leah tilted her face toward him. "I'm here now."

"Yeah, and you haven't run away to Australia."

She tsked. "No way. I love you, Justin. No one else."

His smile grew wider, if that was even possible. "Babe, I love you more."

She laughed. "Good." Leah slipped her hands behind his neck and pulled his face closer.

Their lips brushed once, and he leaned in and kissed her again. He studied her eyes, even though they were blurry at a close distance. The connection between them was tangible.

"I've waited years for this day—to call you mine. You're special to me."

Leah answered him with another kiss, but this time her mouth lingered over his, and he responded by showing her the passion he'd held back for so long. His hands threaded into her wavy hair, and his hand cupped her cheek. He held her more delicately than a precious ceramic purifier—like she was a treasure and full of purity. He wouldn't break her heart or her trust in him. He would value Leah for the rest of their lives.

CHAPTER EIGHTEEN

Ten months later ...

Justin took the paddle from Hannah. "Thanks for doing this after hours."

Dusk had settled across the lake, creating a peaceful and still night. Cicadas chanted their song.

"No problem at all. Especially if this leads to what I think it might lead to." Hannah gave Justin a mischievous smirk. "That's why I gave you my pink kayak. Pink is for 'love is in the air.'" She sang the last few words.

He held a finger to his lips. "Shh. She might hear you."

Leah sat in the kayak below, oblivious to Hannah's teasing.

Justin climbed down the jetty ladder and carefully placed one foot at a time into the kayak. Leah gazed at him with loving eyes. Maybe she did know what was about to happen, and she seemed happy about it.

"Ready?" he asked.

"As ready as I'll ever be." A generous smile broke free.

Yep. She knew. And he was fine with that.

He took the paddle and stroked side to side while Leah

leaned back, facing away from him. Maybe he should have rented a canoe so they could have faced each other.

Gentle ripples formed across the lake as the sun sank lower on the horizon. He wanted her to take all this in. He often sensed God in nature more than in a church building. Justin wanted God's blessing on their new season in life. This was his way of acknowledging Him—enjoying creation and the gift of finding a soulmate here on earth.

The quiet breeze fingered Leah's hair, and her profile silhouetted as she faced the mountains. A faint reflection cast an image of the horizon over the far side of the lake.

It wasn't long before they made it to their destination. Would Leah be surprised? The kayak slid into the sandbank, and Leah held onto the side.

"Stay there for a moment. I'll drag the boat in, so you don't have to get your shoes wet." He stepped out in his flip-flops, and sludge oozed between his toes. Yuck. Better him than her.

Justin hoisted the kayak as he moved backward. Leah giggled as she rocked side to side from the movement. He hoped to hear that laugh for the rest of his life.

Justin grinned and offered her a hand. "My lady, please disembark."

She placed her hand in his. The ground was still a little soft, so in one swift movement, he threaded his free arm around her back, let go of her hand, and scooped her from under her knees like a bride—or a bride-to-be … if all went well tonight.

The motion released more laughter from Leah. "Justin. Don't you dare slip and drop me in that mud."

"Never." He pretended to lose his grip for a second.

She squealed and smacked his chest. "Not funny."

He carried her to dry ground but didn't put her down. They wove through some trees, and the picnic layout was precisely how he'd imagined it would look in the early evening.

Leah gasped.

Fairy lights lit up the perimeter of the blanket, and sunflowers were scattered on top. Two cast-iron chairs sat on either side of a white table dressed in white linen, silverware, and domed servers.

"Justin," she whispered. "This is gorgeous."

He lowered her legs, and she stood on the grass.

Leah turned into him and rested her arms over his shoulders. "You're so thoughtful."

He gazed down at her. "I am thoughtful. My thoughts are full of you. Always." He kissed her nose before stepping back and lacing his fingers with hers. He led her to the table and pulled back a chair. "Please, take a seat."

She sat, and he inched her chair toward the table.

A rustle came from behind them, and Leah startled. Right on cue, Marcus appeared in his waiter attire, and a cloth napkin draped over his arm.

"Oh my gosh." Leah put a hand to her chest. "What on earth are you doing here?" She laughed. "In Trinity Lakes."

Marcus chuckled. "I have returned." He looked at Justin. "We decided to keep it a secret and surprise you. We're doing it right this time." He winked.

Leah looked between the men. "Okaaay."

Justin took his place at the table. "Relax. Enjoy."

Marcus stepped forward and took the chilled bottle from the wine cooler. "And this is sparkling water from Italy. You can read the label if you like."

She waved a hand. "It's fine." She chuckled. "I trust you both don't want to give me the wrong stuff. We all know I can't handle even a sip of alcohol, and we've learned our lesson."

Marcus's laughter echoed out to the lake. He poured water into her wine glass.

Leah tilted her head. "Seriously, Marcus. What are you doing back in the States?"

He poured sparkling water into Justin's glass. "A couple of

things. First, to revisit my American mates." He nodded between them. "I also obtained a working visa. I'll be here for a few months. Got a job at the country club." Marcus shrugged. "I'm open to new opportunities."

Leah took a sip of her drink. "Well, it's good to see you here again."

"I picked Marcus up from the airport last night. He's staying at the country club—accommodation is included in his package." Justin brushed the back of Leah's hand with the pad of his thumb.

"Nice." Leah turned and met Justin's gaze. The smile in her eyes said she'd always choose him, every time. He didn't have to worry about her having feelings for Marcus in the past or present.

Marcus placed cloth napkins on their laps before lifting the silver domes. Steam snaked into the night air. The candle in the center flickered over the amazing food. Grilled salmon, fresh, asparagus, baby carrots, and greens filled both plates.

Marcus stood back and pointed his thumb over his shoulder. "I'm just gonna sit in the rental car for a while. Justin can text me when you're ready for dessert."

Leah blinked. "Oh. Okay. Thanks for serving us."

"I love cooking and serving people. Friends even more so. Enjoy." He bowed and backed away, and leaves crunched under his shoes.

Justin took Leah's other hand in his. "Shall we pray?"

Leah nodded and closed her eyes.

"Father God, bless this food, this beautiful evening, this stunning woman at this table, and our future together. Be the center of our relationship as we honor you each day. Amen." Justin opened his eyes and found Leah watching him. Her smile was contagious.

"What's making you smile?" he asked.

Leah darted her gaze to the table, smiled, and shrugged. "I'm just happy." Her eyes locked onto his. "Happy to be with you. That was a touching prayer. I loved the words, 'our future together.'"

He cupped her hand in his. "Do you want a future together?"

She smiled shyly. "What are you asking?"

He smiled. "You were never the patient one, were you?"

Leah laughed and shook her head. She pressed his hand to her lips. "I can't wait any longer, now I know."

"How long have you known?"

"All week."

"I'm that obvious, am I?" He chuckled.

Leah nodded.

Justin placed the domes over the food and stood. "Okay. This wasn't how I planned it, but here goes." He moved to her side and got on one knee. Justin dug into his inside pocket, which had a hidden zip. He jiggled the inner pocket open and retrieved the jewelry box. Would he remember the words he'd practiced? It didn't matter. Speaking from the heart was best.

Leah gazed down at him with expectation. Gentle light flickered over her face.

"Leah, I don't know when I fell in love with you, but it was years ago. We started as friends and worked well as a team back then, and my admiration for you grew with each passing year. I didn't think I was good enough for you."

Leah shook her head and smiled. "You know better now, don't you?"

"Yes. We are equals. I know who I am—far from perfect, but teachable enough to grow. I want to embark on this journey in life with you. I love you deeply, Leah Thompson. What do you say about changing your last name to mine?"

She tilted her head back and released a joyful laugh. Leah dipped her chin. "How about this?" Leah got out of her seat and mirrored his position on one knee, placing her hand on his. "Since we are equals, this seems right to me." She smiled. "I love you too, Justin. I will always choose you—to love you forever as my soul mate."

He lifted Leah's hand to his lips. He flipped the box open with the thumb of his other hand and tried to get the ring out with his fingers. The box and the ring tumbled to the blanket.

Justin squinted at the space between them. "Oh, man. This isn't how it's meant to go."

She laughed. "It's fine. Shall I get a phone to shine a flashlight?"

Justin palmed the blanket, searching for the ring. He touched the box but couldn't feel what he needed. Leah felt around the picnic blanket too.

"Try not to move too much. It should be right here." Justin's heart quickened. The shadows of the trees were blocking the moonlight. He turned and smacked into something hard.

"Ouch!" Leah fell back.

"Oh my gosh. Sorry, baby." Justin crawled to her, leaned over, and rubbed his thumb on Leah's forehead. He gave the injury a quick kiss.

A light shone over them. "How are you guy's doing?" Footsteps crunched the ground nearby. "Oh, sorry, mate. My bad timing," Marcus said.

Justin jumped to his feet. "No. It's perfect timing. I need that light. We lost the ring."

Leah sat up, rubbing her head. "Excuse me? Who lost the ring?"

Marcus chuckled. "Mate, it's already starting."

Justin squinted at the light shining in his eyes. "What's that?"

"I don't know much about the Bible, but I know the bit where Adam blames Eve, and this kind of looks like a garden."

Justin belly laughed and snatched the flashlight. "Gimme

that." He shone it over the blanket. Within two seconds, he'd spotted the diamond. Good thing he bought a huge one. He scooped up the ring and pulled Leah to standing. She brushed dried grass from her clothes.

Justin mock-glared at Marcus. "If you're gonna stand there, maybe you can record this?"

"Nah, mate. You're gonna smooch her after the ring goes on. I know how this goes." He lifted his palms and walked backward into the shadows.

Justin faced Leah and smiled. "We better get this on before *I* lose it again."

"You're a fast learner. You did say you were teachable."

"Yeah, I hear the woman is always right."

Leah wriggled her finger. "You better believe it."

Justin chuckled and slipped the diamond onto her finger. Leah jumped into his arms and pressed her mouth to his.

He stumbled back a step, keeping Leah in a tight embrace, and laughed under her lips. "Such enthusiasm."

"Mmm hmm." She mumbled. "I've been waiting ten months for this day."

Their kisses turned from playful to passionate, an explosion of happiness at finally committing their lives to each other.

Justin cupped her cheek and rested his forehead against hers. "Thanks for choosing me."

"There was no other one besides you." Leah gazed into his eyes.

A yelp in the woods made them both flinch. Marcus? "Oh, I have his flashlight."

Leah burst into laughter, and Justin joined her. This was the funniest proposal he'd heard of. It would make a great story for the grandkids one day.

Justin hugged Leah and moved her into a slow dance, swaying side to side. He pressed his cheek to hers, and they danced in the moonlight shining over Lake Wainscott. In his opinion, this was the perfect proposal. Nothing could ruin this night when he held the girl of his dreams with his ring on her finger.

EPILOGUE

One year later ...

Leah tentatively climbed the thick rope. She peeked up at Justin, who clung higher on the tree with his bare feet firmly in the grooves. He reached out a hand and wriggled his fingers. "You're nearly there. Don't look down."

Leah smelled certain death if she slipped, and the stench of her sweat was embarrassing. She needed to jump in the lake to get free of body odor. Yuck.

Her heart pounded in her ears. The bark was dry and brittle against her feet, and the rope chafed her hand.

Leah took a deep breath. She could do this. The entire summer camp stood crowded on the bank of the lake. As the youth leaders, Justin and Leah must show their adventurous side. Justin seemed to have no problem. He thrived on moments like jumping off ropes at epic heights into a lake.

Below her, the clapping of hands grew into a rhythm. The sound multiplied, and a chant as well. "Leah, Leah, Leah."

Justin grinned. "No going back now. You can't disappoint the kids. Come on, Mrs. Perry. We'll do this together."

Ever since they'd married and returned from their honeymoon, it had been adventure after adventure leading the youth group together and becoming a team. She hadn't known how much she'd be stretched. Marriage had fast-forwarded her maturity, but at the same time, she felt young and vibrant with the journey they embarked on together.

Leah wedged her toes into the next groove of the trunk and pushed herself up. She latched onto Justin's hand. His firm and secure grip held her tight, like how he'd captured her heart. With ease, he led her to his level. She placed the massive knot between her knees and twisted her legs around the rough rope.

"How are we going to do this again?" Her voice came out breathy.

Justin ran his teeth over his bottom lip. "How I envisioned it in my mind isn't exactly going to work."

That didn't sound promising.

Justin swung her around to face him. Leah squealed as she wobbled.

"How about I sit on the opposite side, and we hold one hand? On the count of three, we jump off, and in mid-air, we push away from each other."

Leah nodded.

"But you need to trust me and let go at the same time. Hold your arm out straight, and we'll do a safety jump into the lake."

Her pulse thrummed in her throat. "Okay, that should work."

Justin straddled the rope, lightly sitting on her legs. He used one foot to push away from the trunk and gain momentum. He gave her a reassuring smile, and nervousness fled at that moment. Life with Justin would never become boring.

He pushed off the tree, and with a swish of the swing, the rope creaked above them. Cheers and chants came from below, but all Leah could do was stare into Justin's blue eyes, reflecting from the sun. She laughed as her tummy tickled with spasms.

"Three, two, one. Let go!" Justin called.

Leah unlocked her legs, held tight to Justin's hand, and

straightened her arm. She focused on the sparkling lake. Her hair floated past her ears as the wind rushed over her cheeks.

A squeal of delight came out in full force. "Aaargh!"

Her feet hit the water first, and her body was enveloped in cool water. She blew air from her mouth and blinked.

Justin took her other hand as they floated to the surface. His smile caused bubbles to float from his mouth, and he mumbled something. Her ears cleared from an air pocket.

He repeated the muffled words, "I love you."

They broke through to the surface of the lake. Leah shook her hair and gasped in air. She wrapped her arms around his shoulders as he embraced her waist. She kissed his cheek and whispered, "I love you too."

He kissed her forehead and swung her to face the youth group. They lifted their joined hands like champions. "We did it!"

A collective cheer rose from the kids. Beaming faces and smiles made Leah's heart soar. She turned into Justin's arms again, allowing him to hold her afloat in the lake. The sun on her skin and the water at her feet made her feel alive. And the man holding her held her heart and wouldn't let her go this time.

She'd always choose him.

ALSO IN THE TRINITY LAKES SERIES

Book #4 Always By My Side by Iola Goulton

Tabitha Thomas longs to leave Trinity Lakes and travel the world in honor of her grandmother who raised her. But she's needed at home—she's the responsible triplet who stayed home to run the family inn while her brother and sister left to live their dreams.

Kiwi, Logan Wylde, doesn't call any place home. When an injury frustrates his travel plans, he accepts an invitation to return to Trinity Lakes and recuperate at the Lakeview Inn, where he hopes to rediscover his purpose in life. What he discovers is an attractive host who has a mystery to solve.

Available May 2023

Now available

Book#1 - **Never Find Another You** by Narelle Atkins
Book #2 - **The Ocean Between Us** by Meredith Resce
A charming small-town, contemporary romance series

ABOUT THE AUTHOR

Lisa Renee is a member of Omega Writers, Australia. She adores babies enough to have seven of her own. Lisa breeds Ragdoll cats now instead of breeding humans, waiting until her adult children start to multiply. She lives in Australia, enjoying every moment of writing, publishing, and podcasting.

ALSO BY LISA RENEE

Single Again Series

More Than a Second Chance

Acres of Promise

Polarized Love

No Filter

Bachelors of Clear Creek Series

Fake Engagement Mistake

Fake Identity at Stake

Caught in the Act

About Time You Proposed

About Time You Noticed

Bachelorettes of Clear Creek Series

Faking it for Gran's Sake

Brielle and her Man Trap

Visit www.lisareneeauthor.com for a free novella when you join Lisa's newsletter.